CAPTIVATING SHORT STORIES

DEBORAH ANNA

INDIA • SINGAPORE • MALAYSIA

ISBN 979-8-89322-873-1

CONTENTS

1. The Empty Room 5
2. The Fosters.....9
3. Taking A Risk 13
4. An Illness.....17
5. Fly! Fly! Fly! 21
6. Escaping The Torment 25
7. Closure 28
8. My Angel 32
9. Losing A Friend 35
10. Trapped.....41
11. Land of Milk and Honey 45
12. The Transformation.....51
13. The Panic Chamber 55
14. Between The Devil and The Deep Blue Sea.....60
15. Torn 64
16. Escape.....68
17. Treasure 72
18. IGOR.....76

19. Not Normal 80

20. Fate 83

21. Tabby 89

22. Kisha 93

23. The Estate 100

24. Sigatoka 104

25. No Use 108

26. Brothers 112

27. Delights Can Turn Sour 116

28. The Unknown Should Never Be Ventured 119

29. The Mission-Possible 123

30. Why 127

1. THE EMPTY ROOM

The cold, metallic touch of the door handle brimmed at my fingertips, a sign of long absence. The interior was dim, the air dark and sweet and musky. Shuffling my feet over to the window, the smell of old laundry detergent, a faint smell of body spray from the local dollar store, and the settled fizz of a carbonated drink washed over me and rolled out the door, like the fleeting moment of the ebbing of a wave slapping against a treacherous storm escapes, dissolving into amphorae and grain sacks.

Pushing the window open, the sticky edges voiced a shrill melody as sunlight carried and settled itself on every corner it could reach. Outside, crisp copper leaves swayed gently in the wind, and the nimbostratus clouds overlapped one another, painting the sky a gloomy grey. The shaggy autumnal decrepitude, dishevelled beauty in gold and scarlet, came once every year, Pete's favourite.

The room, alive with the song of the wind and the kiss of sunlight, was the polar opposite of Pete's hospital room- daunting cream-coloured walls, fashioned with mundane medical posters that housed my brother, the beeping of his chemotherapy machine, and the brave indomitable smile my parents tried to plaster onto the sorrowful scab that was implanted onto their face. I reached for the bed. The marsh-reed ticking of the mattress crackled softly beneath me, rubbing its thin fingers against my back while I stalked the area, eyes heavy behind my head as I tried to imagine the missing pieces of the room back in its spot. Pete had requested everything in his room- ranging from his prized action figures to the guitar my hands so idly became calloused on- to be placed in the garage. "It does not feel right to leave my things here without me," he had said, a guileless grin etched upon his face. The bed did not fit the garage, though.

The bright orange of the leaves caught my eyes once again, perhaps my mind hoping for a chance of succour. Nevertheless, my chest felt strangely hollow. Just last year, Pete was here, drowning himself in the autumn leaves, eyes bright in the firelight, his face drawn sharply by the flickering sunlight that coloured his fawn skin golden. I touched the thought like a bruise, testing its ache.

Just last year, Pete was healthy. My mind rummaged through broken fragments of memories of the past year, finally landing on a rather heart-tugging one: the poignant moment before Pete had to leave for the hospital. He sat in this very room, fingers strumming the strings of his guitar, displacing all my thoughts. The marriage of melodies resounded through was pure and sweet as water, bright as lemons. It had warmth as a fire does, a texture and weight like polished ivory; it buoyed and soothed at once. "I will be alright," Pete smiled, the skin at the corners of his eyes crinkled like a leaf held to flame. His resolve was always certainly admirable.

The memories well up like spring water faster than I can hold them back. They do not come as words but like dreams, rising as the scent from the rain-wet earth cascaded through the deep recesses, invading my most cherished thoughts. The pinpricks of stars and the pacing course of the moon outside the window were the only light now. I blinked until I could see it, even when I closed my eyes. The yellow curve brightened against the dark of my eyelids as I thought of the final memory: Pete's hand, limp in mine as he spoke his last words to me. He was like a flint, a spark away from fire - and when he died, he lay pale on the bed, never to feel excruciating pain anymore. All things swift and beautiful and bright were buried with him.

As I sauntered through the hallway the next day, I grimaced as I always used to an automatic response whenever there were audible, stifled groans and moans reverberating from the room, grating on my auditory senses. Now, there was silence. The room was empty, but all his belongings remained, as his Mother could not bring herself to remove even one item. It stood with placidity, quietude never experienced before.

Then I heard it: the humming. I could have sworn that there were quiet strummings of a guitar, but when I sprinted to check, all I could see were his favourite pyjamas inside out.

2. THE FOSTERS

A fiery red orb of light slowly sank beneath the horizon, and threads of light lingered in the sky, mingling with the rolling clouds, dyeing the heavens first orange, then red, then dark blue as I watched with a wavering gaze. "Dinner is ready!" a clear voice, followed by my foster Mother's massive body obstructing my view of the brilliant sunset as my eyes tore away from it. I would not be here much longer, though.

"Sally! There you are!" my 'mum,' Corine, exclaimed. I sat on the rosy cedar-brown chair and stole a quick glance at Patrick - the other foster child. As usual, he had his earphones in, hidden by the overgrown golden locks of hair at his side, drowning out the conversations made at the table as metal music blasted through his eardrums. He was aloof and nonchalant about everything-typical of a teenage boy.

Above Patrick proudly stood a picture frame of my foster Mother and father and their late daughter, Marina. I was old enough to notice what Corine was doing. She sought solace in me, dressing me up in the same manner as Marina used to, forcing me into the hobbies her beloved one used to enjoy; she was shaping me into the embodiment of her as if I was stone and she was a sculptor.

Everything seemed peaceful, and pleasantries were exchanged when necessary, but I was also old enough to notice the silent stares of my foster father, Mr. Edward. Something had always felt terribly amiss when 'Dad' was around. His eyes would peer my way, and this scared away every last bit of comfort in me. Blue flecked with grey. Corine never seemed to notice - she was always distracted, fixated on other ways to sculpt me into her perfect child. Although Patrick noticed, he did not seem to care, but on some occasions, he would stare closely at the one-sided bond between us as if pondering about something. But he may have just been daydreaming; I would not know either way as he never spoke - selectively mute.

The last straw was when, one Thursday afternoon, my drawers had been pulled wide open with some of its contents blatantly removed - immediately suspecting 'Dad'. It had been practically proven to be true when I caught him lurking around the hallway soon after. He had always looked as if choked by words, like they were crowded in his mouth, threatening to spill out at any moment;

they never did. His hands were always squirming and fidgeting, too.

The house was suffocating; a broadening sinister effect, it made me have dreams that left me lying awake at night, bleary and bloodshot. The almost screams that scraped my throat as I swallowed them down. The way the stars turned and turned through the night above my unsleeping eyes. "I have to leave." the thought occurred again; a surety rose in me, lodged in my throat.

After dinner, the duffel bag containing only the bare essentials awaited me. It did not have to wait any longer when the Sun fully sank beneath the horizon, melting away as stygian darkness took over the sky. My feet dashed out the front door into the forest behind the house, never to be found again. The ominous forest was a creaking shack created by nature to serve as a reminder that things could always be much, much worse. The bleak yet choking thick mist that swirled and surrounded me was the first thing that spoke of an eerie feeling; vast silence reigned over the land as tendrils of fog uncurled around my feet with every step taken.

Then, the snapping of a twig, not from me. My pupils dilated, the beating of my heart ringing in my ears as my feet twisted around. 'Dad' stood there amidst the darkness, outlined by the creaking, whispering dark spruce tree. My mind screamed at me to bolt, but my feet felt as if they were anchored down by the twisting vines; I was riveted to the spot.

He muttered some hardly coherent words, but I slowly made them out. "Patrick, Patrick is... not who you think he is," he whispered, barely audible, but still the sound carried; all my senses came together, searching for ridicule, the scorpion's tail in his words. It suddenly dawned on me all the staring and missing objects. Dad was telling the truth. "He's..he murdered his own father when he was eight years old!"

I gasped and was flabbergasted, but my eyes diverted their view to something behind him. Golden and gleaming hair, shining as bright as the sharp, metallic object in his hands. It was too late. I tried to warn him as I blurted out, "Look out!" He swung around to see Patrick, who stood right behind him, then shifted- an infinitesimal movement, towards him. His cheeks stretched, and grinning sinisterly from ear to ear as the long axe swiftly came down on 'Dad.' "Do you think that you can send me away?"

3. TAKING A RISK

After what seemed like days of cascading through broken branches and overgrown vines, I had finally reached the beach. “You have two fully functioning legs and arms, and yet you refuse to do anything outside of your room!” my sister, Mable, spat. I had felt guilty, knowing that she had been wheelchair-bound since birth and having to watch me skim through life without a care for my physical health. So when I remembered the beach Mable, and I used to go to it with Father and Mother, it was not too far from home and was a famous place for divers within the area. I felt compelled to visit it once again, to show my elder sister that I was capable of more and allow her to live vicariously through me.

Out here, everything seemed different. There was nothing quite like the thrill of digging my toes into gritty sand, feeling it nip hard on my heels as I stared out into inky-black water. Mother and I wheeled Mable out to a spot and gave her some food and magazines. The sea stretched out into an abyss, melting into a velvet puddle as it rippled along the reflection of a brilliant, lonely sunset. I stretched my thumb out towards the sky- outlined against the painted stars, Polaris sat on the tip of it- and breathed in. Saltwater, as usual. Waved bravely at Mable before breathing in the fresh sea air.

I put on the diving gear that I had found at the back of the garage and rushed towards the sea. The saltwater blurred my vision and made my eyes flood until I cried tears of ocean water. It was almost like fear in the way it filled me, rising in my chest, how swiftly it came: buoyant where they were heavy, bright where they were dull. I did not know how to put on the goggles correctly, but I ignored it. Venturing deeper into icy, obsidian water, I skimmed my palm over the waves' hissing bubbles. My mind went into autopilot; it was too late to regret anything. I dived deeper into the water with my eyes wide open past the promontory.

Underneath the surface's black sheen was a world I could barely comprehend. The water was a deep, cerulean blue; shoals of iridescent fish swam by as though entranced by a mystical force. Although my ears were deafened by the firm press of seawater, I could hear the mellow bubbling of the ocean as though it was a slumbering creature. The most breathtaking view, however, were the jellyfish. "Squishy soft squids!" Mable used to call them. They floated away gently, bobbing their slender tentacles as though dancing to an invisible tune. It was their ghostly glow, brazenly purple against their spider-silk bodies, that enchanted me.

Abruptly, just as quickly as I had dived in, the landscape changed. Jellyfish become rounded, rotten plastic bags. The water turned into slick oil, and the ocean floor disappeared beneath my feet. The tar filled up my lungs, the grease clogged my nostrils, and all I could do was taste its bitter liquid against my tongue as my vision became blurry while my hands gesticulated sporadically. I opened my mouth to cough and scream for help, but the oil quickly seeped into my sockets and down my throat. Grasping at the water but to no avail. Slowly, I drifted off.

I woke up coughing out bloody but black phlegm. Someone hurriedly brought me a metallic pan to spit into, and I gasped in sync with the beeping of my heart monitor. A doctor was called to drain the fluid in my lungs, and I sat back with tears prickling in my eyes. “Calm down for us, Sally!” the doctor’s words echoed, my mind just barely processing anything being said. My ears picked up on the nurses’ pitied murmuring that a girl with no previous experience nor training should not be diving alone. I heard hoarse whispers and a heated argument between the Mother and the doctors.

Pondering upon that for a moment, I brushed my hands longingly along my white, clinical bedsheets, but images of the squishy soft squids appeared bobbing up and down amidst sea horses, along small anglerfish enveloped by darkness in my head. Only then did I realise that my eyes were opened wide, but I could not see.

4. AN ILLNESS

"We are sorry, ma'am, but we cannot let you enter yet," the chief of neurosurgery informed me as my eyes pulled away from the linoleum floor, taking one last look at the room in front of me; my Mother on the surgical bed encapsulated by suffocating white walls, decorated with natural images in colours as bright as glacier melt-water offspring flowers that held up incisive tools waiting to be doused in blood.

The palms of my hands gripped the icy metal doorknob one last time before letting go. I staggered to the back of the waiting room, awaiting the convalescent: grieving spouses, anxious fathers, and even elated families holding onto bright helium balloons rich in colours that contrasted the static white of the building - all waiting for their relatives to be discharged.

The atmosphere outside the building seemed to complement the one inside. The sky screamed a colour of misty grey as rolls of clouds appeared to have perfectly blended in with it, signalling the start of a stormy night, or at least that was what it looked like from the rosy cedar browns married to the iron that curved into the great arms of a chair in which I sat, pondering the events of the past few months.

It had started just a mere few months ago, a seemingly ordinary call with my Mother. Even over the phone, it was noticeable how she had become disconnected, lacked appetite, and had an ineptitude to follow a conversation; not thinking too much of it, I brushed it off and assumed she had just felt the signs of ageing. It was not until much later when my phone rang to alert me of a call from our long-time local store manager, calling to tell me about my disorientated Mother wandering the parking lot after getting groceries and claiming to not have any knowledge of her whereabouts or how she had arrived there. That was when something felt truly amiss. How could my Mother forget a place she resided in for over thirty years? She seemed distant and preoccupied, somewhat pensive.

I was adamant to get to the bottom of this. Much to my Mother's annoyance and defensiveness, yet long stares into my eyes, her attempts to drown me with the words "I'm fine" proved to be a futile attempt as I dragged her to the hospital in search of an explanation.

A clock stood sentinel at the corner of the room, the golden pendulum making its way forward and backwards rhythmically as it practically begged me to look. Three hours had passed, it seemed. The once-occupied room now held a fragmented memory of the people who were once here, empty and stoic. As I turned to look outside, familiar with the surroundings somehow, the foggy grey had dissolved into a velvet black, as bold streaks of light pulsed through the graphite sky, illuminating the brilliant pathway above for a split second before reverberating a monstrous roar, and in turn came the rush of rainwater.

The quick pattering of footsteps made my head snap back to the hallway, which now held a doctor dressed in an oversized surgical coat. In front of him was a striking blue medical file, and he made his way purposefully towards me.

"Your Mother's results are quite common for her age..." He then proceeded to peer intently while asking me a totally redundant question, I thought. "How have you been? I've taken the liberty to speak to your family about sharing my concerns about you." Behind him stood my brothers and Mother with tears streaming down her face. Startled as he opened the results of the X-ray of my brain. I was flabbergasted. All I found out was that, recently, I had been abnormally forgetful. So they obviously took tests, but I had absolutely no recollection.

Results were indicative of a pituitary tumour. The room swirled around me. Mother broke down, unable to contain it anymore. I finally comprehended all her strange antics. Her inability to behave normally. "My suspicions... were they right? I was beside myself, my precious Jenna!" She blurted out finally and sobbed uncontrollably, inconsolable and feeling disorientated. No wonder. The actions of a doting Mother.

5. FLY! FLY! FLY!

Shane stared stoically at the forest that was a stone's throw away from his house. The abnormal, thick fog that swirled and twisted on the forest floor alerted him of an unexplainable eerie feeling. The sound of the creatures that blended in the forest created a melody when heard in unison, signalling a possible impending doom. The leaves of autumnal colours rustled while whispering softly to one another.

Shane noticed a decomposed carrion- a dead animal sprawled on the wet floor of the forest. It released an unpleasant stench that mingled with the air. This marriage of smells nauseated him.

It happened two years ago. Shane was an active child; the young boy was elated and content with his life. He often ran around the house frolicking with a game of tag or hide-and-seek alongside his adorable three-year-old sister, Elena. Needless to say, they were the perfect pair of siblings.

Shane was always oblivious towards his surroundings- so inattentive that he was unaware of the threats enclosed around him. The ball he was playing with rolled over to the grass across the road. He knew that it was too risky to go outside, but temptation allured him towards it. Unfortunately, his body collided with the front bumper of a silver-polished Mercedes, sending Shane into immediate unconsciousness. This tragic accident was, however, merely inevitable due to his immaturity and nonchalance.

From that day onwards, he was unable to make full use of his bodily functions. What used to be two active legs are now just two objects protruding from him, and he felt as if his spine was impinged in his wheelchair. Those pale, lifeless limbs no longer supported him; they might as well be discarded. He couldn't fathom how the accident occurred, and he could've sworn the vehicle that hit him was his father's car. That was all he remembered. Strangely, whenever he questioned the true incident, they would always turn away crestfallen. No one spoke of his father either.

Slowly, the gust of insanity consumed him as the months passed by indolently. With no sustenance or distraction, days blurred into a singular stretch of infinity. The malicious sky morphed between a scorching heat and piercing cold, between light and darkness. It was late summer, and it did not rain, but it wouldn't have mattered to the seemingly lifeless child.

His Mother, a slender, exiguous lady, looked after him. She did everything she had to do as if it was a daily routine for her. He glared outside the windowsill from the second floor, where the sounds of joy and laughter arose. Elena always sang: "You can fly, Shane. Come on. Just fly," and this only enticed him more and more. He did not see a purpose to remain alive; being paralysed neck-down tormented his mindset. Words barely escape his mouth, and he only replies in monosyllables when being asked questions.

Elena often repeated what she said to him. An innocent four-year-old kid, perhaps nothing else better to do than to confront her older brother in a wheelchair with, "You can fly". Those words had a meaning to it, though. If he jumped, would he really fly? That was the question he frequently asked himself. Despite being eminently tempted to jump, he was diffident and apprehensive of the consequences. Many phases of daytime gradually passed by, and his urge and desire to jump increased rapidly until, one day, he finally obtained the courage to do so. After all, what else was there to lose? His body couldn't function anymore, leaving him in misery in a wheelchair.

Elena was down below with her head tilted upwards, excited to envisage her brother's attempt to fly. Perhaps it was his cowardliness that made him constrain himself at the very last moment. Sadly, it was too late when he felt a pair of frigid hands pressed on his lower back. "I'm so sorry, sweetheart," a small voice shuddered perturbingly. "You're exhausting! It's too late to change your mind now!" A sputter of breath. A whisper of a plea for help as he lay sprawled on the front lawn.

"Mommy, is he going to fly like you said?" Elena asked while peering at her brother. Her cute voice was overshadowed by the last loud breath of anguish, dismay, and disarray, which slowly progressed to the demise of her brother that lay before her.

"Yes, dear. Shane is flying with Daddy now."

6. ESCAPING THE TORMENT

The sound of creaking floorboards echoed through the house as a frail, gaunt figure emerged from the shadows, illuminated by the flickering light of a nearby lamp. With slow and deliberate movement, she lifted her scrawny, brittle finger to her moulding lips, signalling for silence. Her voice was as gentle as the delicate susurrations of the wind in the trees.

Heavy footsteps suddenly struck the room, plunging it into darkness and dread. The children's giggles abruptly ceased, replaced by shaken whimpers. We knew the cue: Dad was home. I quickly grabbed my siblings and led them under the table as a bolt of lightning cast a shadowy silhouette of a ruthless beast from behind the tablecloth. We held our breaths, waiting it out. Lights flickered with each step, the stomps grew louder before they finally faded away, and the bedroom door slammed shut. My heart sank as the fear for my Mother.

My siblings returned to their toys. Meanwhile, I sat on the stairs in an attempt to listen for my

Mother's voice; silence awfully prevailed, leaving my mind racing with fear. Until a gentle twist of the doorknob dispelled my fears. "Mama!" I cried, I embraced her tightly, desperate for reassurance.

She led us to the kitchen and poured us juice, assuring us that our father was asleep. Contrasting her soothing demeanour, I noticed blood trickling down her thighs, which had dark confusion, and she quickly wiped it away.

"I wish he'd never wake up… or that he would just leave!" My sister's innocent voice trembled. My Mother sat down, pale-faced and lips trembling. The chill haze of her fear began to crystallise as she took a long, hard look at the faces of her four terrified children.

As dark skies loomed overhead, my Mother snuck into my room. Sitting against the wall, I furrowed my eyebrows in an attempt to decipher her unfamiliar expression. She gingerly stroked my auburn hair as it cascaded down my shoulders. Her forced smile stretched from ear to ear. "I have a plan," she said as I wiped away her tears. She explained that she had found a domestic violence shelter and would leave immediately to ensure its safety before returning for us within a few hours. She handed me a crumpled note with an address written on it and paced back and forth as she laid out the details of the plan.

A few hours excruciatingly turned into days. Feeling sick with worry I snuck out and made my way to the address on the note, hoping to find her there. I looked down at the note and back up at the dilapidated building, uncertain what I would find inside.

The abundance of the drunken men left me questioning the supposed safety of this shelter; my stomach twisted. Amidst the reek of vodka and foul men, I searched desperately for my Mother. Room by room, floor by floor, until I finally found her. She seemed different, sitting there, with unfamiliar soulless eyes and scantily dressed. I approached her, my voice breaking; she remained unresponsive, probably from being heavily drugged, as tears streamed down her flushed bony cheek. I noticed the necrosis of her fingernails. All of a sudden, I was interrupted by a lecherous man who abruptly threw me out, shouting to her that her client had arrived.

I lay helpless on the floor and through my tears, watching him mercilessly slam the door shut, sealing my Mother's fate and ours.

7. CLOSURE

Shadowed by an ombre of melancholy hues, a stranger sat alone on an ochre park bench parallel to a liquid mirror in the form of a tarn. It reflected the alloyed tones of the dusking amber sky like a mock painting, hoping to someday appear as depthless as the horizon. He was a vapid silhouette of depression; he sucked in the air behind his teeth, absorbing the mellow scent of petrichor, and hissed out a burdened sigh.

Only a day earlier, there was a torrential downpour and a lowered casket. He remembered the years spent at a barely breathing bedside, the decision to end life support, and the echo of a flatline in a white room. Her silver curls lay strewn across the featherdown pillow, framing her face like a perfect halo. Pamela would be an angel soon. "George," she whispered, reaching out with waning strength to grasp his freckled hand, "promise me you'll do it?" A sinking feeling clutched him like a humid cloak, his lips curving into a gentle smile as a single tear slipped down his ageing visage. "I promise." He had to sacrifice all those years ago, his own infant child, as an expense in extending his wife's lifespan; when the bills for treatment began to accumulate, he knew that he would not be able to provide for her. The only solution was adoption.

Isolated, he had only time to ruminate like a watch set anticlockwise. Tick, tick, ticking in reverse through every moment passed in his lifetime. Pamela's dying wish was a near-impossible task, a feat that seemed to increase exponentially as he approached the door for the third time that day. He had written to her a few days ago, but there has been no response yet. To visit and attempt to rekindle my relationship with my own daughter, someone I gave up, was an excruciating and painful task.

Yet, as he lifted his hand towards the oakwood surface, it trembled, and he could not bring himself to knock. So, he left, retreating to anyone's common sanctuary, the neighbourhood park. Slowly, I sat down on a bench, sadly, made for a pair.

Reeling him out from an ocean of grief was a young woman pushing a stroller through the park. Observing with keen interest, his gaze softened as he saw her lifting the golden-haired child up and out of the pram into her cradling arms. At the sight of his heart, he felt a chronic weight on his conscience that would never leave him.

Tears welled up as he watched this male toddler gurgle as his Mother dangled a supposed favourite toy above his head. He could not but only procure a gentle smile, and all past regrets were momentarily dissipated. He started daydreaming long after the woman left, only acknowledging the beginnings of dawn when his own hands were stained in a twilight flush. However, as he moved to leave, he marked a fluorescent blur in the grass. Nearly unnoticeable, shrouded in the shadow of a nearby bush, was the baby's toy. An unexplainable fondness overcame him as he held the plushie and put it into his coat pocket. It protruded, looking awkward, but he didn't mind, feeling placated strangely by a mere stuffed toy.

George stood on the same threshold once again, this time with an inspired air of assuredness, not daunted. His eyebrows creased in worry. Gripping with trepidation, he imagined Pamela to alleviate the anxiety and anticipation. He knew that he had to fulfil the vow he made to her… her last and dying wish …to rekindle with their once abandoned daughter. With a hollow sigh, he knocked. The door swung open. Standing there was the same woman from the park.

"Oh my, I've been looking for that everywhere!" she gasped, reaching to grab it from his pocket with one hand while the other hand was balancing a drooling baby. She stared at his stunned expression. "Thank you for finding it, Mr…" she trailed. He glanced at the child and could hardly conceal his shock as he met the baby's hazel gaze; an uncanny resemblance… Pamela's eyes... He was moved to tears. Then, all of a sudden, she sighed as if she knew the truth and had accepted it. "Come in, please… Father?" she queried, beaming. Stepping across the threshold, he felt a wave of relief as he began a new start.

Only now, it dawned upon him that the reason for Pamela's request was because she foresaw that he would be all alone. It was not for closure but for his new beginning.

8. MY ANGEL

I peered out the shattered window at the slushy and whiteout snow. Dark spruce forest frowned on either side of the frozen waterway. The trees had been stripped by a recent wind of their white covering of frost, and they seemed to lean toward each other, black and ominous, in the fading light. A vast silence reigned over the land. Everything outside the musty window, from the size of an atom to the size of the sky, was mundane and recognisable to me. I felt like punching the window and forcing my way out, but my wheelchair incapacitated me.

Suddenly, an obnoxious sound saying, "Mr Lim, Mr. Lim," barked at one of the nurses, and immediately, two others shoved a plethora of rainbow-coloured pills and a glass of water. I wheeled myself to the white linen sheets, slowly drifting off to sleep.

The cacophony of bells reverberated through the hall and jolted me out of bed, infuriating me as the nurse bellowed, "The men- your sons- are at the front door asking for you." Two forlorn-looking gentlemen sauntered in. I was perplexed, and my mind instantly went blank. I could not recall their faces. I was downcast as I could not recognise my own sons?! They then proceeded to pull out umpteen legal documents pertaining to my estate, claiming that they needed prompt attention or else I would stand the risk of losing my precious assets. They were fastidious and explicit about exactly where to sign. My initial response was that I had no clue about the legal ramifications and was extremely hesitant, but they assured me, while pacing up and down, that it was a mere technical issue that only required one signature, and all would be well.

All of a sudden, the tintinnabulation of the doorbell shook me from my state of perplexity. The door creaked open. Mary! Finally, a face I could recall. She confronted them, and they tried hard to justify their actions. They alleged that I had the desire to bequeath my entire legacy to them because of some dealings a few years ago.

Mary immediately grabbed the pens and broke them into minute pieces. They tried to escape, but Mary was ahead of them, with two security guards that were alerted beforehand. They were swiftly taken to the authorities, and I was placated by Mary, my sweet, beautiful angel- Mary, as she stroked my face gently.

She wheeled me back to my humble abode, my safe haven, my room, and continued to stare stoically at the television. I thought for a while- Does it matter if I don't know who she is? Mary says that she has always known me and that she deserves it all. I tried to look for answers as I gazed out of the window. All the trees were tightly knit, signifying that life, in all forms, appeared to look like they were connected in more ways than we can understand yet were equally divided in a myriad of ways. The scent of earth and water drifted, wafted, and permeated through the air.

Her soothing voice tried to say that I should transfer everything to her. I could not resist that mesmerising face just after she gave me the only source of reprieve, the only thing that removed my anxiety and emptiness. I felt calm after that. She says that every time she gives me this vitamin. It's labelled 'Psychedelics'.

9. LOSING A FRIEND

I observed with an unwavering gaze as a fiery red orb of light slowly sank beneath the horizon, and threads of light lingered in the sky, mingling with the rolling clouds, dyeing the heavens first orange, then red, then dark blue until all that was left of the sunset was a chalky mauve and then that melted away in turn as stygian darkness took over the sky. The day was long, and the colour of the sky did not matter to me because I was with Laila, my best friend. The truth is, I have known her all my whole life. We were inseparable neighbours, like two peas in a pod. I have a lot of affection for her because we have lived through many hardships together.

Through thick and thin, undoubtedly, she had always been there for me whenever I needed her, even though she had a miserable, lonely life. Her parents divorced when she was only eight years old. After the custody battle was over, her father moved to China permanently, leaving her Mother, who had to single-handedly support her. She missed her father terribly. Due to the lack of funds, her Mother had to work day and night. She hardly had a family life that she yearned for, and that was why she often spent time with us just to fill the void. She often said that our friendship was the only thing that kept her going.

Conversely, this is not an ordinary friendship. The things we have done together I dare not even divulge, but if I don't, I will explode as I cannot contain it any longer. How could I possibly describe my quirky friend? Well, to be honest, she was an extremely boisterous, energetic, yet passionate girl. Whenever we went to the park, her ears would pick-up sounds of animals in distress. She would then teach me how to personally nurse them until they were well enough to fend for themselves. She had even rescued a bird that had fallen out from a nest in a tree. Her empathy for animals was indeed touching, and it really made an impact on my life.

Having said that, her compassionate nature was not confined to animals. However, she was selective about who she wanted to help, and of course, I was the first on the list, as our friendship was inextricable. One day, my water bottle accidentally spilt into my bag. All my books got wet. I was petrified because Ms. Sarah, my science teacher, waltzed into the classroom like a seething dragon, glaring at all with bloodshot eyes. Within seconds, she wrote my name on her science book and shoved it into my hands. She then grabbed my soaking-wet book. Ms Sarah, who was walking around to check, was livid to see Laila's hands clutching the wet textbook. She bellowed at her and then commanded that she go straight to detention. She duly submitted, but before slinking out of the room, she winked at me and put her finger to her lips, leaving me aghast!

This kind of reckless yet selfless sacrificial act went on for years until, one day, she received a letter from her father in China. Her eyes lit up when she burst into the room and read the letter to me. She told me that her father had invited her to go to China to live with him and his new family. It seemed that her father had remarried, and he now had a new baby boy. I took the news in slowly, trying to digest everything, but then she dropped the bombshell on me. "Do you think I should go?" I stared at her in disbelief and hesitated for a while. Tears welled up in my eyes, and I clenched my fists behind my back as I was unable to respond to her. In my mind, I shouted many reasons for her not to leave, but should I be standing in her way? I was really happy for her.

However, my heart sank because I was going to lose my dearest friend. Let's face it, she will not be able to keep in touch. The fact is, she is going to be lost in China by the crowds of people. Why would she need me anymore? I harboured selfish feelings and wanted to tell her many frightening stories about stepmothers and slave trades and any other morbid stories that I could think about, but instead, all I uttered was, "OF COURSE YOU SHOULD GO!"

Within weeks, she had packed everything and booked her flight. Everything passed by me, and before I knew it, I found myself in my airport with her Mother, who was sobbing uncontrollably. We all said our goodbyes and our farewells before she turned towards the escalator. After that, I went home and just plopped on the bed and went to sleep. Suddenly. I was then rudely awakened by a loud whisper, and I decided to see what the commotion was about. Apparently, the plane my closest friend was on had gone off course and was now missing!

I began to shriek, terrified that my best friend was gone forever! Pacing the floor to and fro while wringing my hands, I tried to figure out how this could be happening. My parents tried their best to calm me down, but to no avail. It was hopeless. I imagined all kinds of horrific scenes that made my heart palpitate even more. This went on for hours. I flicked through all the channels for more news and was infuriated when I was met with disappointment. I bawled and became inconsolable when the newscaster announced that the plane was nowhere to be found. I then became delirious and fainted from sheer exhaustion.

Hours later, I slowly opened my tear-dried eyes and convinced myself that it was just a horrible nightmare. I then stormed into the hall, demanding my handphone. I wanted to call her, but my sister looked sadly back at me, jolting me into reality. Was she gone forever? Why did I let her go? Was it all my fault? If only I had been adamant that she stayed back. She would have agreed with me in a heartbeat. Deep down, I knew that I was being extremely selfish and immature, but I didn't care. All of a sudden, my younger brother raced into the room, screaming at the top of his lungs! "They found them!"

I jumped towards the television just in time to see the Prime Minister announce that the plane had to divert to an island because of a malfunction, and due to the bad weather, they were unable to contact anyone. He further assured the public that all the passengers were accounted for and were safe and sound. They were on their way to their intended destination. The newscaster did not mention the details. Tears of joy flooded my cheeks as my family members danced around with me jubilantly. My best friend was alive!

After two hours, the phone rang. It was her! I was ecstatic, but the line was static, and I only heard her distinctly say, "You know, all I could think of was you...but.... but you wanted me to go away, right?" Then there was a crackle, and the phone went dead. My mind raced, wondering what had gone wrong. Then the phone rang again. This time it was the police. They said, "I'm sorry to inform you that Ms. Laila died from an overdose before entering the plane."

10. TRAPPED

Crouched under the sink, I shivered uncontrollably from the cold, harsh wind that was ferocious and unrelenting, dreading the thought of returning to that alcoholic, deranged, sadistic man. The school bell had rung hours ago; classes had terminated long before dusk. I had waited too long in the lavatory. I was now trapped. I did not leave the school premises on time, resulting in a lockdown. Perhaps it was better to be isolated and behind bars in a school than to be in a loveless home filled with torment and despair.

Peering out the window, one could see that it was sunset. I observed a fiery red orb emanating streaks of dim yellow light while dancing across the horizon. Threads of light lingered in the sky but slowly faded away, vanishing before my very eyes. Thus, the defiant sky is adorned with white patches of forlorn clouds. The wind whistled a sonnet, making me feel nostalgic as I thought of my late Mother. From where I lay, I had the perfect view of the Sun dipping behind the crest of the mountains, the sky awash and a blaze with colours found at the heart of a fire. The rest was dove grey with a subtle hint of purple, just enough to announce the coming sunset, which left me feeling trapped.

I had purposely stayed back in school to avoid him! His intoxication had reached a new level. I wanted to avoid him at all costs. I didn't have a concrete plan but was thinking of hiding until I found some money to get on a bus to anywhere but that insufferable house. He would often berate me publicly, shouting at the top of his voice like an egomaniac. He judged me meticulously without once taking my feelings into account. Everything I did was ridiculed. To make matters worse, he even invited drug dealers over, and that made me squirm. But where could I go? I'm underaged and have absolutely no money.

Apprehensive as I was about my next move, I mustered up sufficient courage to venture into the unknown. The empty corridors beckoned towards me as if they knew I was coming. The welcoming committee of doors opened their arms gleefully, signifying a warm embrace. They were dust-ridden but hid the classrooms perfectly. The atmosphere did not resemble a school anymore; it just paraded like an empty house awaiting the master. As I had all the time in the world, I ambled across the hallway towards the pantry. Aggravated by the delay in the consumption of food, my stomach grumbled and growled. The ravenous god of the belly was not placated by mere tap water. So, I grabbed open the pantry door to see an array of delectable delights. Was I really trapped, or did I want to be? Gluttony could not begin to describe the way food had gone through my gullet.

Disgusted by my unhealthy binge, I decided to go to the school's sports complex to work out. Lately, I have been obsessed with food because it gives me comfort. Anything that would take my mind off that decrepit, incorrigible evil man who is the bane of my existence. The thorn in my side that is relentless made me feel eternally trapped.

The court floor glistened under the moonlight that streamed through the windows. The squeaky clean court screamed and screeched every time I stomped on it, indicating its displeasure as if it knew I was an unwelcome visitor. I didn't care, as I needed to vent! The net loomed above me. I was rather minuscule compared to my peers. A few balls lay scattered around the court, beckoning towards me, wanting me to play with them. They were taunting me, strangely, but I felt wanted for the first time. I reluctantly attempted a few dribbles but failed miserably. I scurried out of there, not wanting to remind myself of yet another reason not to live, feeling no solace in anything.

As I trudged down the hallway, I came across the science lab, which released a pungent smell of noxious ammonia. Perhaps it was the last experiment conducted that day. The grotesque concoction of chemicals, coupled with my overloaded stomach, made me nauseous. So, I made my way to the infirmary. As soon as my head touched the pillow, sleep overtook me.

I was awoken by blaring sirens. They've come to retrieve me. How did he know??? I detest- no, loathe- going back! That's not my home! But neither is this school nor anywhere else in the world. Whether I went back or ran away with empty pockets- either way, I was trapped!

11. LAND OF MILK AND HONEY

As I gazed above, the sky was blue, only sporting a few wisps of white clouds. They formed almost neat lines above, being dragged by a wind I could not feel. I wandered among the debris in a street ravaged by bomb blasts in a once bustling city in a war-torn humble abode.

All I could vaguely recall was being thrown against the wall of the building as the ceilings crumbled before my very eyes. The deafening sounds were incomprehensible; they reverberated through the room. I woke up with a blurred vision, not knowing how long I had been out. Gripping the sides of the wall, I tried to gain my composure but stumbled to the ground. Balancing was an arduous task.

As I forced myself onto my feet, refusing to give up, I got a glance of the outside world through what was left of the partly demolished wall. The jagged-edged glass from the fragmented window shattered against the cracked concrete flooring. With my hands cut and bleeding, I staggered out of the ruins.

Immediately, my eyes welled up with tears, and I grimaced as I watched my husband cradle the motionless corpse of my firstborn – Ahmed. My knees buckled as I fell to the ground, wailing at the top of my lungs; I crawled towards him and held my child for the last time. I'd had enough of this chaos, distraught by destruction; did I have to wait for everyone I love to die in front of me? Within minutes, we buried our sweet, precious son amongst the other numerous victims of this abomination. This catastrophe left us speechless. The misery it has caused us is beyond comprehension. It was then that I made up my mind. For years, many spoke of the boat to the Promised Land, and it was a mere dream for us. However, today, I was told that this was going to become a reality.

I sprinted towards what was left of my humble abode, which were only unrecognisable remnants. However, that did not deter me from plodding on to retrieve all my belongings. My husband clutched the palms of my two children. Aisha; meaning 'life' and Armaan; meaning 'hope.' We glanced quickly at our home, knowing we would never see it again.

We were told that there was only one boat left going out because the other boats had already departed and were never coming back. We scurried towards the last dilapidated, dingy, decrepit boat. Judging from the outer appearance, one would think twice about boarding this overburdened, pathetic lump of rusty metal. However, without hesitation, we scrambled towards it, clutching the children by their hands.

There was an ear-piercing scream like someone had lost their mind in the midst of hardship. Out of nowhere, an elbow jutted against my temple and my vision blurred instantaneously. I groped around for a few seconds until it reverted back to normal; despite the atrocities, we could not give up and finally made it aboard.

We huddled together in the cold, harsh winds; 'crammed' was an understatement. The children sat on us, as there was no space between each person, perhaps only a centimetre. Only when Aisha let out a cry of hunger it dawned upon me that we did not bring a single ounce of food with us. Amidst the helter-skelter, we had failed to realise that the journey would take weeks on end. My stomach began to groan, not due to hunger but at the thought of all of us starving to death despite being on the verge of freedom.

My thoughts of self-pity were interrupted by loud wailing from land as the boat gradually drifted away; turning my head, I could witness the misery of the remaining discards. The memories of the expressions they wore would be etched in my mind for the rest of my life.

They were aghast; they had not expected to be left behind. They came to the realisation that this was their last hope for freedom. Arms flailing, some leapt into the dark, murky waters. The dangers that loomed beneath them did not deter them. Our flight was on the way while theirs was terminated not by choice, but by fate. If we had been a few seconds late, we would have shared their impending doom.

The journey was smooth sailing in the beginning, but soon, fights ensued between the passengers. Some were dissatisfied by the lack of space while others began mini-feuds for insignificant reasons. Days passed with no food and no water, and my children lay limp in my arms, looking lifeless. All of a sudden, a man who had been observing us peered at us and shouted, "They're dead! Throw them off!" I let out a scream like a banshee. I retorted, "No! They're just sleeping!" I could hear murmuring influencing the others. Soon, there was chanting; in the blink of an eye, my husband leapt into the choppy waters of the sea, sacrificing himself for our family. His sorrowful eyes met mine, and it said a thousand words. The trauma was overwhelming as I collapsed and fell unconscious.

I jolted out of my semi-comatose state to the cheering. The journey was over. I leapt up, but my head swooned. I looked down enthusiastically to find Armaan and Aisha asleep, pale-faced and with eyes shut tightly. I tugged at their sleeves; then it hit me. They were no more than skeletal remains. With this last straw that broke the camel's back, I let out a screech which resembled a banshee with every ounce of my being as I was unable to contain any more torment. No one even looked at me as each was deaf- refusing to hear the cries of others when they each felt the excruciating pain within.

I was beside myself, drifting with the crowd, moving but clueless and completely lost but still clutching on to their lifeless bodies, hoping against all odds. Everyone alighted, and I followed suit like an animal into the slaughterhouse. Although the unadulterated beach and luscious greens were a welcoming sight, I felt hollow inside.

We trudged on the beach, and the crackling of seashells underfoot brought back the sound of the crackling fire. In the distance, a raven crowed. It sat upon a broken tree stump, which resembled a gravestone and stared at us with curiosity. I looked carefully around the area for some sign of relief, but instead, I saw a line of army officers, each holding a rifle, pointing at us.

My mind was racing.... "Is this the Promised Land?"

12. THE TRANSFORMATION

Oyugi, a frizzy-haired, angular teenager whose arms resembled a bifurcate tree, felt dejected while ambling languidly in the forest that was decorated by a rainbow of rich, autumnal colours. The strange cloud swirled around the trees, creating the perfect ambience. He was forlorn as he contemplated the way his peers mocked him whenever he failed to kill the hunted animal. They would taunt and ridicule him repeatedly, making him feel so humiliated.

He couldn't help it and would often be stricken with grief when even the smallest creature lay limp in his hands. His attention was diverted by trees which were swaying from left to right in an enlightening web of life.

The smell of the rain was permeated with a whiff of the grim reaper, intermingled with odours that arose from the roots of goutweed and rhubarbs. Discombobulated by the recent events coupled with disdain, he tripped and soon found himself rolling helplessly down a hill with arms divaricated. A small bush broke his fall, and he grappled with the twigs around him to stand. Strangely, to his consternation, he sighted the much sought-after Amur sable, a roan antelope, but he was not certain if it was a Hippotraginae, which was much inferior to the Yakutsk and Transbaikalian. He shuddered because this reminded him of Sable Arabia, which honoured Diana, the queen of witches.

He was astonished to find himself in front of an opening to a cave of impenetrable blackness. His shadow blended with the cave, which was overlain with obsidian and pumice. A glimpse of light from the end of the cave attracted his attention as he made his way there, taking extreme precautions, through the unknown abyss. There lay a magnificent talisman in the shape of a 'chowke,' which was a hunting knife, perched on a stone, illuminating a strong orange glow. Mesmerised by its mysterious aura, Akeem gingerly cradled it and claimed it to be his own.

In time, he became strangely avaricious as he used his newfound power for things unimaginable. Soon, he started to demonstrate his unique abilities during the hunt. He and his members crouched behind blades of grass privily, intending to snare, observing rabbits and hares. He swiftly pounced on his prey and used the 'chokwe' to decapitate it. A surge of virility entered his spirit, and he absorbed the spirit of each distinctive creature. The others gaped in awe and disbelief.

He soon found confidence and progressed to bulls, deers, boars and antelopes. He extracted the essence from every creature and transformed it accordingly. He even had the audacity to tackle elephants swiftly without any effort. The mixtures from these animals allowed him to gain magical powers beyond measure. Everyone gaped in awe. However, these thrills were momentary, and he got tired of these 'easy' prey.

Insatiable, he transcended to the highest on the food chain: predators, mutilating wolves, tigers and even lions, while embracing every ounce of their stealth and physical prowess- their basic instinctive nature to mutilate. His appetite became unquenchable, and he yearned for more. One morning, after the last dismembered animal was discarded by him, he decided that he needed more.

Late that evening, before the sunset, he crouched under the bushes, whispering incoherent words hoarsely under his breath. All ran helter-skelter, shrieking in trepidation, when finally he looked at them with venom in his eyes, softly chanting,

"Vengeance is in my heart, death in my hand, blood and revenge are hammering in my head, but I will give you all a head start!"

13. THE PANIC CHAMBER

The piercing ultraviolet light was thankfully engulfed by the beclouded fluffy white cotton balls high up in the sky. Chirps of a cacophony of birds were heard as they flew around, bringing truth to the phrase, 'early birds get the worms.' However, for Diane she heedlessly did not care for the worms at all. Despite inheriting the grandiloquent and bijou estates that were often peered by the covetous gleam of society, she felt her stomach burn with acid at the thought of how a picture-perfect family lived felicitously not long ago, and now they were six feet under. Being orphaned was not part of her plan. But life often throws curveballs, and you are just instantaneously hit. Nevertheless, she started her day by fixating her vacant gaze on the lush foliage and greenery surrounding the perimeter, wishing to be free without a care of the world like those hummingbirds jovially chirp and chit.

She was bequeathed her beloved family's opulent heirlooms on top of the exorbitantly prized treasures, which meant that she never had to work another day for the rest of her life.

She opted to roam aimlessly around the burgeoning stalls, as the smells of confectionery sweets wafting in the air as it, mixed with the greasy fat diffusing from the fast food chains. She loved the fourth avenue, especially since that was where she met her darling love, Adam. Here, she was reminded of 'Troilus and Cressida' - For to be wise and love exceeds man's might.

One dazzling afternoon, he entered the café, and she accidentally spilt coffee all over his briefcase. He was such a gentleman that he just laughed it off, and they instantaneously hit it off. He was an enormous man, always prim and proper, giving an ostentatious feeling as he was dressed in a designer suit, pressed to perfection with golden-rimmed glasses, and sat perched atop his perfectly carved nose bridge. The Sun broke through a thousand years worth of cloud and finally radiated its luminescence on her. He was her Camelot. He was her duvet of comfort and warmth; hands always warm around her cheeks as he would softly placate her. She was incandescently happy.

He was a victorious businessman, running a highly lucrative investment firm. Adam was godsent! He had been nothing short of nurturing and gentle to her since they first clapped eyes at each other. She felt alive for the first time in months, unlike her usual melancholic, forlorn self. She was in a state of total euphoria. Perhaps due to resentment and her innate rebellious nature, she agreed to move in almost immediately. Her fears were placated by his splendiferous four-storey-high mansion filled with portraits and etchings of famous painters such as Picasso and Rembrandt.

They were birds of a feather who flocked together as he had revealed that he, too, was an orphan. They had both decided to take it slow and move her things one at a time since he knew how easily perturbed she got. She was hesitant at first to bring all her diamonds, but then, upon seeing the alarm system, she was immediately convinced that all would be well. During the house tour, he revealed that the house was equipped with a 'panic chamber' for emergencies. Diane let out a silent chortle, knowing just how conscientious he was. A few weeks later, she became very much at home in this abode.

However, one strange night, they were awoken from their slumber by the tintinnabulations coming from downstairs. They both sprung out of bed to check the CCTV and were horror-stricken by the sight of four masked men clad with weaponry raiding the living room. Paralysed with fear, Adam dragged her to the chamber through the secret passageway from their bedroom. She sat in silence, eyes rheumy, while her beloved tried to comfort her. Once it was eerily silent, Adam tried hard to assuage all her fears but made the chilling decision to investigate.

Minutes turned to hours before it had dawned on a new day. Could he have been abducted by these malefeasants? Diane was ill at ease and at wit's end. Perplexed and mortified, she relented and decided to venture out. As she gingerly opened the door and crept upstairs, she was about to witness an abomination. Empty. It was utterly empty, void of beings and objects due to the raiding. All her family heirlooms disappeared!

Adam, she feared, was kidnapped. She alerted the authorities. As they arrived, they started their intense investigation, insisting on his photograph in order to alert the other officers.

Lo and behold! As they traced his identity, they realised that Adam did not own the house. It belonged to a Swedish couple who were away on business. Adam did not own a successful investment firm. In fact, Adam did not exist. This thief was a wanted man by Interpol on accounts for a plethora of robberies and burglaries. She was dumbfounded. "The mansion isn't his?" she queried, hoping against all hope, realising that all her jewellery was gone!

"No, madam, I think you should prepare to leave as now you are an intruder."

14. BETWEEN THE DEVIL AND THE DEEP BLUE SEA

The luminous light bulb in the lamp started flickering and buzzing as my feeble hand started to cramp due to the perpetual hours of incessant note-taking. Abruptly, my dorm room door gushed open - it was my roommate Stella. The malodorous stench of alcohol permeated through the air. She then yammered about how I needed to cease burrowing my head through the gargantuan anatomy textbook. I scoffed as I had to endure her idiosyncrasy and irksome antics since exams were only three weeks away.

My phone alarm started to ring, reminding me that it was time for my night shift. Stella and I scurried off to the hospital for our shift as we grabbed our babushkas. Walking to the hospital, it was a gloomy night with enigmatic clouds hovering around the crescent moon with colossal chartreuse trees around the vicinity of the pathway to the hospital. As we entered the hospital, its walls were leaden with a bold red stripe, causing the ambience in the hospital to be melancholy. Coughings from patients would ricochet off the walls and echo throughout the hospital. Furious eyebrows and upside-down smiles were painted across the nurses' faces. As I began my shift around the wards, I halted at the medical supply room to restock prescriptions onto my steely cart. Rummaging through a drawer abundant in bright neon orange pill bottles, a striking sapphire blue pill bottle emerged. Picking up the bottle to meticulously read the description label, I discovered a small reprieve: a drug that had been banned in this conservative hospital a year ago. I thought to myself how studying would be a breeze with this drug. I would pass the exam with flying colours and not be seen as a failure in my parent's eyes since they had spent a fortune on my nursing education. I then duplicitously slipped the blue lapis bottle into my pocket and carried on my rounds around the ward.

Peering at the bottle, I was in a trance. Contemplating on whether I should indulge in the pill or not. I was desperate not to be viewed as a burden by my parents, so I gulped the pill down with a sip of my Zavarka and began studying immensely. After three days of digesting the pill, Anas, my other roommate, leaked shrouded news to me - a urine test would be conducted two weeks before the exams. My heart dropped dead silent. My lips quivered hysterically as beads of perspiration formed at the top of my head. As Anas left to diffuse the astonishing news, Sylvia came into the room to see a frenzied nurse, me. I was hyperventilating heavily, and my palms turned clammy. Sylvia questioned if I was alright, and I confessed that I had been using drugs to study. She looked befuddled as I became harried. She swiftly sprung into action and comforted me by suggesting that I could use her urine sample instead of mine - so my urine appeared clean and drug-free. I felt a little sense of alleviation as I slowly regained my composure.

The day came: the test. We were standing outside of the hospital's bathroom, and the nurse handed Sylvia and me two empty translucent cups. When it was our turn to excrete into the cups in the bathroom, we were being closely examined so no mischievous behaviour was condoned. I concocted an idea of how I could slip my cup sample underneath the bathroom stall. So she slipped the cup back, half full of urine, which was adequate. The mission was a success; we left the bathroom, chuckling in glee at our imminent windfall.

Days had passed after the panic attack. All of a sudden, Anas, with no anticipation, called

Sylvia and I, saying that we were needed at once in the director's office. Making our way to the office, we straightened our hair and outfits. We then entered and faced the director, who had a solicitous expression on his face.

He proceeded to talk about the test results. My heart palpated against my ribs; my breathing frantically became intense. It felt like the entire room was swirling around me. He declared that Sylvia and I were both pregnant! I shook my head in perplexity to then realise that it was she who was pregnant. I glared at her as my eyes were sparkling with fierceness. Allegedly, nurses who are pregnant in this conservative hospital without being married is unacceptable and would have to be automatically expelled.

Streams of tears descended down my cheeks as I was not allowed to confess the fake urine sample, or else I would be expelled too. Remorse struck as a dilemma dawned upon me. It felt like I was stuck between the devil and the deep blue sea.

15. TORN

Starstruck, staring at my dream high school sweetheart in admiration as my heart palpitated against my ribs. Soft blonde hair full of curls cascaded ever so daintily upon her shoulders; her innocent face with majestic splendour captivated me as she sauntered in a phosphorescent sapphire dress. The sparkles glistened like she came out of a fairy tale - a fantasy came true. I swaggered up to her, holding elegant, alluring claret roses with a resplendent smile on my face. An ineffable thrill! On the way to the grand ceremony- high school prom, Lynette sat in the passenger seat as I drove in my Mother's dilapidated vehicle - the only thing my late father had left her while I inherited his opulence.

The luxuriant ceremony was led by a stairway decorated in lustrous palatial crystals. Lynette, coming from an impoverished background, was mesmerised as she had never witnessed such sumptuousness. Elated partners danced on the pulchritudinous grandiose floor of the ballroom to the melodiously deafening contemporary tunes. People stared at her elegance in glorification while they obnoxiously scoffed at me. "No way a goddess actually chose him." My smile faded as I was deprecated. Suddenly, Lynette constricted my arm firmly - pulling me closer. "Shhh. Let's go; I know a better place," she whispered in her euphonious voice, pulling me towards the exit of the flamboyant ballroom, jolting exultantly. She promised that we could escape to a phantasmagorical place. Spirits brightened up as her effulgent smile radiated. The sound of our footsteps reverberated through the desolate, lifeless parking lot as we made our way to the car. Leaving the venue, she compelled directions as we mindlessly cruised, laughing away. Clueless regarding our destination, yet there was a gush of euphoria- only feeling delectation, which affected my focus immensely.

Time passed in a split second. Looking around, I was lost. Surrounded by malady-brown trees, a primordial forest. Centuries-old trees with sprawling limbs guarded the stringent darkness, blotting out any light. Driving uphill in the manual car, struggling with my lack of experience. Her saccharine voice in the background made me forget my fears but left me strangely befuddled. There was an uneasy gut feeling on the inside, contemplating my decisions until we arrived at the very top of a remote, unfathomable hilltop.

The zephyr drifted against my shipshape hair as we stepped out of the vehicle. Her heels tapped against the tar road as she sashayed towards me while her floor-length dress danced with the breeze. I felt her encase my forearm tightly, pulling me to the edge as she turned me around to face the transcendent sight of the busy city, placing her arms around my waist. An enchanting feeling - everything I had ever wished for in my wildest dreams. Suddenly, her voice changed ghastly as I heard a monstrous whisper. "Sorry, I'm torn, I need the money," she muttered in a blood-curdling voice.

As I turned around in mystification, my Mother's presence greeted me spontaneously - with a depraved, formidable grin I wish I could unsee. "You see, dearest, your insufferable father left me a pittance unless you were... not around anymore," she snarled. Lynette proceeded to roughly push me over the edge while my Mother could be heard ensuring the plan was executed until I fell down the ravine with my arms flailing. Now, here I was, numb and paralysed, hanging on to jagged stones with nothing but a sense of betrayal. They peered from the edge, convinced I had died. As I lay helpless on the ground, the unbearable pain in my body could not begin to compare to the heart-wrenching feelings. Before

I closed my eyes, I saw Lynette looking at me. No regret, just blankly staring. I felt like a fool. I should have known getting a dream girl like her was impossible.

Sadly, the thing that gripped my heart the most was that my Mother valued money over her own son.

16. ESCAPE

Our long-awaited escape after living as dolorous disconsolate victims in our own home. My 'Baba,' the man I was supposed to call father, subjected us to lashes from the whip and umpteen unwarranted slaps across her pale countenance. The formidable memory has been embedded into my memory. He was a sinister man who was constantly intoxicated and staggered home at odd hours of the night, with me quivering hearing Mother's stifled shrieks of terror when he committed unspeakable atrocities. I crouched under the bed night after night, waiting for that insufferable man to pass out after he had finished berating us, spewing his litany of profanities.

The final straw was when he raised his hand to lambaste my unborn sister, making her resolute about her immutable decision, fleeing for good. This was an arduous step, but the execrable abuse was unbearable. The escape was imperative. We left everything and bolted for the door after he left for his usual drinking spree. We were determined to never look back. We felt freedom for the first time in years! Ah! The burden was lifted!

The potent scent emanating from the earth and water drifted through the dispiriting forest. Crisp copper leaves swayed in the zephyr. Fortresses of wood surrounded us; primordial trees stretched away from the crinkly floor amidst the bristles of wispy moss. A pulchritudinous cerulean celestial current curved while alluring butterflies fluttered through the rays of the fiery crimson orb.

Our bodies ached under the blistering Sun. My short limbs struggled to carry me any further; my stomach was in knots from agonising hunger and dehydration after hours of walking, and the acid gnawed away at my insides. After drinking the dew from the leaves, we decided to stay there and soon made a small hut using sticks and leaves. I must admit it didn't look too shabby!

Hours and hours later, as I foraged close by for berries, I stumbled and fell to the uneven ground, collapsing in exhaustion. My Mother sighed in tribulation, holding on to her pregnant belly- she was in her first trimester. I sat on the dead fallen leaves of the deciduous forest, fatigued. Unexpectedly, her selfless, benevolent heart had made up its mind. She elucidated, with her saccharine voice, that she would venture for food alone for the both of us as we were starving after three long days with barely anything to eat. She strictly instructed me to follow the river if she did not return before sunset. She further explained that she needed me to stay there in case she returned, as we had nowhere else to go. She was confident that there was a small village nearby. I refused to leave her and attempted to encase her forearm to stop her, but my petite body was no match as she insisted, assuring me that we would meet again. She then wandered off, vanishing into the fog.

Trepidation struck. Feeling disconcerted, I imagined the potential gruesome jeopardies of the wilderness my Mother could face. My hands trembled in perturbation, digging my grungy fingernails into my skin. The warbling of birds reverberated, and the wind whistled around, disturbing the leaves. Staring at the sky in solitude, I noticed the nimbostratus clouds morbidly overlapping one another, painting the sky a dreary grey, perhaps an imminent and impending doom. My heart palpitated against my ribs, triggering a primal flight reaction, a tsunami of adrenaline that shot through me.

The worst came; merciless rain crashed down ruthlessly in torrents. I decided I needed her. Without hesitation, I trudged on, following the path of the nearby river in detestable conditions. As I glanced at the ghastly rapids, a familiar sight caught my attention. There it was - my Mother's *dupatta*, her burgundy scarf. I was mortified as I felt my heart shatter with the thought that she was gone! Scurrying, never pausing, with tears of anguish diminishing my vision. I halted, gasping for air. Muffled tintinnabulations of an archaic town bell could be heard. Looking forward, I found myself in a rudimentary village, one straight out of a history book. Fortuitously, the village was not desolate as civilians populated the mystifying village.

A voice came from afar. An old lady called out to me - gesticulating me in my native language as if to signal an exigency. In my enervated state, I sauntered towards her cottage. As I took a step into her home, I let out a deafening, ear-piercing squeal of exhilaration; a gush of euphoria washed over me. It was my Mother! My spirits brightened. We were finally safe- an inexplicable sense of contentment though she was lying on the bed. She appeared as if she was paralysed. Appalling obsidian bruises covered her body, and I just stroked her hair.

For some reason, she was unable to communicate and had an aghast look that indicated that something was wrong. Her eyes furtively darted from left to right. Suddenly, the shadow of a tall, lean figure emerged from the darkness. My heart skipped a beat as I looked up. *Baba*?

17. TREASURE

"I couldn't put it off any longer!" Jonathan shrieked as he urged us to hop off the small boat. He was frustrated as we had wasted days along the Amazon River while following the map on Marcus's hands to uncover the buried treasure that had been buried in a cave. Our feet landed on the wet soil as we embarked on our journey into the jungle. Using our machetes, we hacked and slashed through the myriad of vegetation of the rainforest, navigating around as there was no route to follow. We went around any space available to us as we proceeded deeper into the unknown.

Hours later, we were in a clearing where mountain ranges were towering over us alongside a sharp increase of humidity, as there was a waterfall flowing through the crevasses of the mountains. Up ahead of us was a cave entrance of sorts. Being curious like a small pack of puppies, we ventured towards the entrance. The cave entrance was covered in iridescent moss and crimson red mushrooms alongside an ominous feel to it. We stood right in front of the insertion point, hesitating, contemplating, and evaluating the map in Marcus's hands to verify whether that was the place we were looking for.

We advanced into it, and there was a strong feeling pulling me in. The interior of the cave was extremely quiet and cooling as if someone was running its air conditioners on full blast. As we went deeper into the cave, Marcus whispered to us to halt our expedition, and he pointed his index finger upwards. My face instantly went pale as we saw hundreds of bats right above us, aghast by the sheer number in a single cave opening. While Jonathan was in shock, he stepped backwards, and a 'clack' was heard. What he had done was the greatest blunder that I had seen with my very own eyes. All the bats were awoken from their deep slumber.

They spread their wings and flew all over the cave, letting out endless amounts of screeching and started ramming into us. Filled with fear and panic, we ran into the depths of the cave just to avoid them. We had reached a part where there were a plethora and a myriad of crystalline structures around us, protruding out of the cave walls like razor-sharp blades. As I took a step forward, my foot suddenly sank into the ground. I lost my balance and fell into an opening that had just appeared right in front of me.

My body felt like it was floating for a few milliseconds as I fell into oblivion while my surroundings began to rumble. Alongside that was the ear-piercing screech of metallic parts, bursting my eardrums and putting me into endless amounts of pain. My body slammed onto the floor, and my head began to feel numb while my ears were ringing. Johnathan and Marcus descended into the hole with a rope anchored onto a few of the thick and bulky crystals and gently lifted me upright.

After I regained my composure, my eyes were fixated towards the hallway that was engulfed by the stygian darkness. The sides of the walls suddenly lit up out of nowhere as if they were guiding lights from a lighthouse to a cargo vessel. We stepped forward with courage into the most mysterious hallway. What had awaited us at the end was a treasure room! Looks like my mishap had led us to our fortune! Jonathan darted forward, leaving Marcus and me behind. He took out a pistol from his backpack and pointed it at us, demanding us to turn around and leave as he fired a warning shot at the ceiling of the cave. We were infuriated but relented as we did not know how else to escape alive!

Filled with fear for my dear life, I was frozen at my feet while Marcus forcefully dragged me back to the place where I fell down. Seconds later, a loud explosion was heard while dark and black smoke began to pour out behind us. He must have stepped on some booby trap! Jonathan's greediness had led him to this untimely, inevitable outcome!

A gold coin rolled out of the hallway, tainted with blood, as I signalled Marcus. We managed to carry some of the treasure with us. At that moment, a dark, long figure was seen moving in the thick smoke, menacing closer and closer towards us. It was something we had never seen before in our lives! Someone or something was released from the cave!

18. IGOR

The Sun illuminated the resplendent, dazzling garden. The aroma of the flowers drifted through the zephyr in the garden, full of alluring butterflies flying through the rays of natural light. Arthur and I cruised through the greenhouse, admiring the delicate artificial cerulean stream curving gently through the cultivated plants; we came to a pause and let out a sigh.

Dreadful thoughts of worry jumbled through my mind, reminding me of the enigmatical dilemma that had been occurring the past few weeks. Top high achievers of the school disappeared one by one, withdrawing from their education after falling sick or being brutally injured. Were they being abused? Poisoned? Nobody knew. Strangely, only Igor, known as the genius, was remarkably unharmed by the mysterious ordeal. Emma was the virtuoso of the school but had vanished just a few days ago. Not to mention the top athlete, Andrew, who had 'accidentally' fallen from the top floor days before his scholarship application results. I swallowed heavily with the deplorable memory of their disappearance, but anger grew on the inside as my suspicions for Igor intensified.

There he was, playing with rats in the middle of the pavement - emitting a gut-wrenching stench as if he had not showered for days. He just had to ruin such an immaculate setting with just his presence. He picked up the squirming mice and stood up to let us cross. His actions made me tremendously pusillanimous of him. Head filled with white dandruff creepy crawly lice and dressed as if he was homeless despite being affluent enough to be enrolled into such a prestigious and posh institution. We walked by quietly and returned to the main building.

The pulchritudinous chandelier in the lobby of the boarding school glistened; flamboyant, sumptuous, lustrous crystals covered the railings of the stairway. Students flaunted their exorbitant designer clothes and jewellery like it was part of the dress code. The high ceilings, beaming bright lights and atmosphere just screamed wealth. A place Igor did not belong in. As we strolled, Alex elucidated how peculiar of a person Igor was. I was compelled to stay away from him at all times as he was known to be perilous. That was an unnecessary request- I agreed without hesitation. We soon parted ways as Alex left to attend a head prefect meeting. I found myself sauntering mindlessly through the luxuriant hallway in solitude until something stopped me in my tracks.

Suddenly, a pair of burly arms encased my forearm tightly. As I turned back, horror-struck. A massive flood of adrenaline shot through my body like a drug as Igor gripped onto me. A dramatic scene was caused as my reflexes let out a deafening, ear-piercing scream in anxiety and despair. The pits of my stomach churned. Igor hoarsely whispered - beckoning me to follow him. He proceeded to vigorously drag me to his dorm room by the scruff of my neck as I retaliated frantically. I was so sure that this was the end. He shoved me into his dorm and locked the door shut. The state of his room was abominable. Rats scurried through the crinkly mossy floor; the walls were dilapidated. He elucidated that he had no intentions to hurt me but had something crucial to reveal to me. Reaching towards his desk, he fished out an ivory book and threw it towards me. It rang a bell - Arthur's journal.

Skimming through the book in mystification it left me appalled. My heart sank. The spontaneous discovery had answered all the injustice. In it were details on how Arthur had pre-planned the attacks on each and every victim, intelligent ones. This was to eliminate the contenders - so that only he would shine in the end. How cleverly he had planted suspicion on Igor, conveniently.

After a few minutes of being stupefied, I left the room and reluctantly walked to the school office in abhorrence - to surrender the evidence to the headteacher. As I walked, Igor and I exchanged looks, but this time, my apprehension had disappeared and was replaced by guilt.

19. NOT NORMAL

It sounded like a straightforward request. John's Mother compelled him to stay in his room and lock the door every day by 9 pm from when he was a toddler until his teen years. His Mother made sure to drill this rule into his head. She mentioned that there would be a formidable consequence if John ever broke this rule. He assumed that it was just for discipline purposes.

He had had a rather depressing childhood. For as long as he could remember, John would go to bed alone without a simple good night or a bedtime story from his parents, unlike other fortunate kids. Growing up as an only child, the poor boy mostly spent his time playing alone or basically had to beg his parents to spend time with him. John grew up with barely any human interaction as he was lamentably homeschooled; he basically lived in isolation.

Every night, he would go straight up to his bedroom after dinner, and he would not even be allowed to leave to get a glass of water. He felt that it was remarkably unreasonable, but his parents were immoderately harsh despite him already being a 16-year-old teenager. One night,

John was struggling with gruesome insomnia as he tossed around in bed for four hours straight, trying to fall asleep, but nothing worked. He was wide awake, endlessly counting sheep as he lay in silence.

Light scraping and muffled noises suddenly echoed out into the somewhat quiet house. John got up in fear and just sat in his bed for what felt like an eternity as he tried to gather the courage to unlock the door and reconnoitre the source of the mysterious sound which left him mystified. As he slowly walked towards the door, counting his light footsteps, the noise gradually got quieter.

He placed his cold, trembling hands on the doorknob as he was about to commit something that was considered a crime in his household. He unlocked the door and took a step outside. His nostrils were immediately struck by a gut-wrenching stench. His eyes started to adjust to the darkened, macabre hallway. John took a step forward, but before he could walk any further, he bumped into something rather soft but firm.

Slowly looking up, his Mother glared at him with devilish eyes... but that was not her. He was horrified and kept whispering to himself that his Mother was not a monster. Her skin was ghost white, and she looked like a pale corpse. As she held her arm, she held it immensely tight; blood started rolling down her arm. However, what she bled was not blood; it looked like black goo, like she was infected with black venom. She was doing a ritual.

Her clothes had gargantuan splatters of dark black, and her hair looked dead and dried, almost flaky. As he looked up and made eye contact with his Mother, her facial expression changed drastically. It was like she was restraining herself from something. Suddenly, she spoke with a deep, indistinguishable voice.

"Bed, now..." she muttered under her breath.

It sent chills down his spine as she had never spoken to him that way before. John ran back to his room, and his Mother slammed the door shut. He jumped back into bed, shivering in despair, digging his nails into his skin. That was when he knew his parents were not normal…

20. FATE

Two grouchy adults are sulking like teenage students in an old, dilapidated, rustic flat. The sounds of plates smashing reverberated, doors slamming, the utter insufferable turmoil; they went with the sound of madness. Stuck in a hole of debt and poverty as loan sharks threatened their lives all due to Alan's formidable gambling habit. The bitter, ruthless man added more fuel to the fire by having an affair. The poor five-year-old son Roland hid under the sheets day by day to hide from his parent's broken marriage, listening to his Mother's stifled shrieks of terror as the execrable beast raised his hand, leaving countless unwarranted slaps across her pale countenance. A household of just misery.

Nimbostratus clouds coloured the sky a gloomy grey as the noise of the thunder got louder and louder. Pat stared outside of the cracked window of her son's puny bedroom, standing in a pulchritudinous rubescent Chinese bridal gown with a profligate amount of makeup and her hair tied up in a constricted bun. Chuckling with a malevolent smile on her face, blood dripping from her index finger - leaving a grim trail on the cold hard ground. A few steps to the white wall on her left, she wrote on the wall with the blood on her finger - "It's not over, darling."

With her firm arms, she picked up her bruised son, who was fast asleep and made her way to the window. Sitting at the edge of the window, tapping her heels on the outside walls. She took a breath of fresh air and held her breath. One foot out of the window, the other soon followed. Frantic, pusillanimous screams came from the ground below as a loud thump echoed continuously.

Ben rushed to the window as he heard a deafening noise of people screaming from below. He took a look outside the living room window, and there he saw his wife and son on the ground. Covered in blood, they were already dead and gone. He rushed to his son's bedroom only to find blood on the walls and the last note Pat had left for him.

Ben was tormented. He had lost his only family. The next week for him was grievous as he cried alone every night over his late wife and son's death. After a while, he somewhat forgot about their passing as he spent more time with Hilary, a 27-year-old woman who he had been seeing even before the tragedy. The same woman who tore their marriage apart. Hilary made his troubles go away, and soon enough, it was as if nothing had ever happened. As if Ryan never existed. He had basically forgotten about them.

Seven years later, Ben remarried to none other than Hilary and had a son together. They named their son Kyle, and they lived together happily in the same apartment where Pat had committed suicide. Kyle was now six years old, and he had never heard of the past. Everything seemed to be unblemished and peerless. They were a joyous and merry family, and their son was healthy.

One night, at 3 am, Kyle came running to his parent's bedroom. He jumped on the bed and hugged Ben tight as he cried in fear. He was petrified. He was shivering in fear as he tried to catch his breath. Kyle elucidated that his older brother was bullying him late at night. Alan was stunned. He had never told Kyle about his late older brother's existence. He had no idea what Kyle was talking about and assumed it was all in his imagination. Suddenly, Kyle pulled up his long sleeve and showed it to his father. Alan was flabbergasted. He was appalled. Deep into the night, the silvery moon dotted the sky as the light glittered on the ground below.

Shuddering in trepidation and frantically panicking, the helpless boy walked into his parent's room. His vague father was awoken - feeling perplexed, staring at his petrified son struggling to catch his breath. Alan's heart dropped and horror-struck as Daniel elucidated that he felt perturbed at night. Stunned, rethinking his past actions. He then assumed that it was all just his imagination until he pulled up his long sleeve. Alan was flabbergasted and appalled. Obsidian bruises painted his forearm, along with countless deep crimson scratches. There was no other way Kyle would have obtained such bruises unless he had been hit. There was no explanation for this.

He ordered Kyle to stay in the bedroom as he left the room to check the bedroom. He carefully opened the door of the room as he quivered. To his surprise, he didn't find anything. Everything in the room seemed normal, and it was pin-drop silence. He left and returned to his own bedroom. He had fallen asleep on his bed. He did not want to wake him up as he felt that Kyle deserved rest after what he had gone through, therefore, he decided to get sleep on the couch for the night.

Anyhow, he couldn't sleep. The thought of his late son and wife kept crossing his mind. He got up and picked up his late wife's jewellery box. It was her greatest treasure, where she stored all her valuable pieces of accessories. He gently opened the old dusty jewellery box. When he opened the jewellery box, he couldn't believe what was in it. He found a note taped onto Pat's diamond ring. The ring Alan had given to her when he proposed to her countless years ago. He read out the note, and he was horrified once again.

"I said it's not over..." the note said.

He dropped the box on the ground and threw the ring out of the window out of trepidation. He jumped onto the sofa of the living room and covered his face with a pillow. He closed his eyes and tried to forget everything. Once again, he was unable to fall asleep. Hours passed, and he kept the pillow at the same place as he did not want to open his eyes out of anxiety and despair.

It was 8 am, and he suddenly heard his room door open. He tried to ignore it as he was too perplexed to open his eyes. He heard footsteps from Kyle. He was already awake. It was rather peculiar as Kyle used to sleep in late on the weekends. He tried to ignore it as he pretended to be asleep. Suddenly, he heard a scream coming from outside the window.

"THIS IS FOR ROLAND!" yelled Kyle.

Ben immediately dashed to the window only to see his five-year-old son fall to his death, the same way Pat and Roland had died. The last words of Kyle included the name of his older brother, whom Kyle had never even heard of…

21. TABBY

Growing up with cats and dogs, I had gotten used to the sounds of scratching at my door while I slept. Now that I lived alone in this newly purchased home, it was much more unsettling.

Every night at 3 am, I would wake to the sound of muffled grunts and repeated scratching at my door. I was under the impression that Tabby, my neighbour's cat, was unhappy about his feeding arrangements, and initially, I made a note to myself to feed him whenever I could. The next day, I searched high and low for Tabby; when I straightened my back from peering through the bushes, I saw Mr. Felix. He seemed preoccupied about some small issues regarding the garden, but he looked rather disdainful.

Sheepishly, I told him that I was looking for Tabby since I wanted to give him a treat. Immediately, his face fell, and he glared at me. I was taken aback by his countenance. He then muttered that Tabby had been dead for over a week. I stood there dumbfounded. I shouted in disbelief, "No way! I swear I heard Tabby this morning!" He refuted my claims and was adamant that Tabby was indeed dead as he pointed to what looked like a mini-grave on the grass patch. He asserted that I would just have to accept it. I could not believe the words he uttered, for I was sure that it was Tabby that visited me in the night.. Or was it?

The next night, I decided to stay awake to confirm that what I heard was Tabby. I consumed all the necessary food and drinks that would make someone stay up for nights on end. However, due to my exhaustion, I was unable to keep my eyes open, and I drifted off to sleep by 2 am. Soon, I jolted out when I heard the sounds again, this time stronger and louder. It made me wonder whether that was the sound of a cat clawing. I hesitated and made excuses to myself not to check, but soon curiosity got the better of me. I braced myself before I took gingerly steps towards the door. I placed my hand on the doorknob; I turned the knob cautiously and was relieved to find Tabby purring, looking hungrily at me. I was so relieved I whisked him up with one hand and went in search of something for him.

The next morning, I was eager to tell Mr. Felix about his mistake; I was so sure that he would be ecstatic to know the truth. However, when I approached the dingy, dilapidated home of Mr Felix, I felt a sense of wrongness. I dismissed it and went in search of the owner. Instead, I saw an old lady on a rocking chair with a veil covering her dry grey hair. I felt uneasy as I approached her. She had wrinkly old skin. Her neck crooned when she turned to look at me. I croaked, "I'm looking for Mr. Felix... Is he home?" The lady said in a cold voice while shaking her head in disbelief, "My husband has been dead for days now..."

Suddenly, I remembered that when I was buying my house, the seller warned me that someone here had been brutally murdered. I was petrified to the core. If Mr Felix was dead, that meant that I was talking to nobody? My mind was shaken and distorted.

I stayed up all night in fear and in thought of who Mr. Felix really was. Suddenly, there were more scratches at my door, and this time, Tabby was already in the room. What could those scratches be? They were accompanied by deep grunts and eventual knocking on my door. Afraid to open it, I peered out of the side window to see who was on my doorstep. Not knowing what to expect, I finally saw it! The most disturbing figure. It was Mr. Felix, staring at me with unblinking eyes; his body was disfigured, and his arms were held really close to his body. A smile broke on his face, his eyes penetrated my soul. I dived back into the covers of my bed and hoped that everything I saw was my imagination, but suddenly, a silhouette appeared through the sheets, and I could hear heavy breathing through my covers.

22. KISHA

In the midst of the crows squawking above the hug of houses in the green that together made an unornamented but contented village of urban families, which was my residence- a place to live in, but I do not call it my home.

Usually, waking up was a simple task for me. However, taking care of the degenerate drunk man was a complete hassle and toil. I groaned when the first beam of sunlight hit my face. I picked up my alarm clock on my antiquated wooden nightstand that had many visible ill-favoured holes by the obnoxious white ants. I looked around in an attempt to spot the forgotten, supposedly newly hand-made replacement one that was promised by Sukhmal.

A sigh escaped from my blood-scarred mouth, the reset button for my emotions, allowing a response to come that has the benefit of both empathic and logical thought. I arduously got myself up, and next to me was Sukhmal, resembling a pig with the fetid, foul-smelling breath oozing out of his opened mouth. Subsequently, I gently got out in fear of awakening the crotchety, crabby, cranky creature on the grimy bed. As usual,

I grabbed the only long-sleeved, worn-out lengha I had and promptly limped out in the hopes of meeting with my one and only confidant, Kisha, whose husband was the superintendent of the police force. I made friends with her after only a few days after I had moved there. I attempted all I could to give a feeble excuse for my late arrival. I subconsciously pulled down my sleeves longer, but not in time, as the blemish blue-black blots and cuts on both of my arms were revealed.

"What's this?" Kisha's gentle voice expressing deepest concern. I looked up and met her warm honey brown eyes. They seemed to read through my fragmented heart that was already shattered and vanquished. A freshet of lukewarm tears streamed down my ashen cheeks obdurately. The tightening of my throat caught me off guard as realisation soon dawned on me that I could not hold the heartbreak any longer. I fragilely fell to the floor in a dishevelled heap as my grief poured out in a continuous flood of relentless tears. She distraughtly lifted me and caught the attention of the hideous, gruesome, and repugnant marks under the sleeves. Her mouth was agape in shock; it was hard to swallow what she had seen. Some of the marks were fresh from last night when he came home drunk and, as usual, decided to 'show me how to behave as a dutiful wife.' She was incensed and whisked out her phone immediately to tell her husband.

"No! He… he promised he will change, and I'm willing to wait!" I finally blurted out that I loved and forgave him. Tears of sympathy swelled in her crystal eyes, but her hands on my shoulders never stopped caressing. She warmly hugged me in an attempt to calm me down while my body was wracked with an onslaught of sobs and tears. Suddenly, I reminded her that I had taken longer than 30 minutes and feared the worst! My absence would infuriate him, I blurted out. Without hesitation, I rapidly darted my way home. She just stood there transfixed, but her eyes looked like they were prepared to do something drastic.

As I approached the village, panting, I caught a glimpse of a huge throng of villagers encircling my house, muttering, and whispering hoarsely. Their eyes soon fixated on me the moment I stepped closer. In front of me lay a burly body on the floor in a pile of fresh scarlet fluid. The familiar grey shirt with its pocket sewed by me, effortlessly gripped my eyes. I stood rigid in a daze. The police soon started an investigation, and they were eager to take me for further questioning.

They escorted me out of my house, and I was soon brought to the police station, which was located two miles away. The villagers stared at me with absolute incredulity as I looked clueless, hopeless, and helpless. They then locked me up and initiated a litany of boundless interrogations. I dispensed as much information as I possibly could to prove that I had clean hands. After a few hours, I saw Kisha! She interrupted and put a pause to the persistent inquisition as she called Mr. Ishaan, her husband, out. I looked through the lucid glass window to behold her passionate conversation with him. She looked like she was vindicating me with every ounce in her body. A sigh of relief was let out of my weary and dry mouth. The sudden knock on my door broke the unpleasant silence, and I was brought out of the intensively agonising interrogation room. I had goosebumps the split second I witnessed Mr Ishaan stamping on my name as I knew that my time here had finally ended. “Click!” The tight handcuffs on my hands popped off effortlessly.

I looked blankly at Kisha as she embraced me with a warm, affectionate hug. I lay my deadpan face into her shoulders and let out a suppressed and tearless sob. The yellings from Bidon, the new suspect, disrupted my moment of solace. “It wasn’t me, I swear! I don’t know where the jewellery went!" he hollered with all his might while the policemen aggressively shepherded him to the door of the room that I just left.

Actually, last night, Sukmal came home with a vigorous, pungent booze breath and started off pummelling me. As his anger reached its boiling point for me not preparing supper for him, he clenched his fists, and his knuckles turned white with tension. With a swift, controlled motion, he lunged at me, landing a powerful punch square on my jaw. I groaned as the familiar throbbing pain trickled back in with my consciousness. I twitched with my body barely moving, the violet bruises stark against my pale skin.

My body bore the unmistakable signs of a brutal encounter, while my skin resembled a canvas painted with a palette of deep purple, mottled blue, and sickly yellows. Every inch of me was marred by the cruel aftermath of violence, with my arms and legs covered in vivid splotches that seemed to tell a harrowing story of pain and resilience. It was as if the bruises were silent witnesses to a battle I had fought, physically and emotionally. I looked at the shattered mirror and the splintered pieces on the floor. I slowly picked up a piece and was tempted to put an end to the incorrigible mess. The bubble popped as he barked an order to me. "Hide this gold somewhere deep, and make sure Bidon never finds it! I'm not planning to share any bit of these!" he yelled. I was constrained after the last hit on my right leg. An appalling, daunting, and ghastly thought appeared in my tangled mind as he handed over the keys of a fastened chest.

After some effort, an antediluvian, archaic, and antique wooden chest emerged. Superb exhilaration filled me as I forcefully lifted it. With a click of the key I had in my hands, the chest unlocked competently and nobly, revealing the glistening, glowing, and glimmering jewellery. They were adorned with ornate details and gleamed with the lustre of gold. The gemstones of rubies, emeralds, and pearls added a burst of colour and opulence. Each detail was a masterpiece, from the intricately designed setting to the flawless gemstone cuts. These stolen jewellery were not merely adornments; they were heirlooms collected over time by Sukhmal, the robber, of immeasurable worth.

After the police station, I was welcomed home by a herd of villagers expressing their empathy. A bitter smile was portrayed on my blanched face, conveying my appreciation for their concerns just before closing the front door. Without delaying any more time, I expeditiously hurried to the well behind my house without looking questionable. I desperately hauled up the weighty mortar, enfolded with patches of dried blood that I had left out of sight from anyone else earlier this morning. I cautiously observed my surroundings, ensuring that no one else was present as I quietly made my way back into the house. Subsequently, I burdensomely moved the bed away and drew out a shovel, ready to begin an incessant digging. A huge wicked grin split across my jubilant face as I relocated the treasures into a bag, easier to carry away, and desperately packed my belongings. After this, I will surreptitiously leave without a trace. I exhaustedly lay on my bed that, was finally free to toss and turn, and soon fell into a deep slumber despite the stinging pain from all the beatings. It did not matter to me. All it took was a swift hit on the temple with a mortar, and he was dead!

All the hassle was worth it…convincing this imbecile of a husband to move into the very neighbourhood where the superintendent of police lived so that I could befriend his wife! All I needed was a gullible 'connected' woman to pour out my troubles to, and the rest would so easily fall into place. I sighed as I would certainly miss Kisha, but not enough to tell her the real truth. I had planned every single detail meticulously! I pondered, slowly drifting off to sleep.

23. THE ESTATE

I returned to the place where it all started – the Burlington Estate. The mansion loomed proudly over the marble fountain that stood sophisticatedly in the circular driveway, gurgling aggressively in the quaint night. The lawn mown to perfection, smatters of white petunias peppered among the green as crickets chirped a symphony. I smoothed the creases on my pants as I exhaled, nervousness bubbling in my stomach. Knocking on the door of the colossal structure, I hastily tucked loose tendrils of ginger hair behind my ear as the extravagant timber doors were pulled open. A haughty-looking woman stood at the threshold with her cold, grey eyes squinted, inspecting me from head to toe, then proceeded to turn on her heel after barking an order at me.

Growing up fatherless was always challenging. What was even more exigent was to know absolutely nothing of the man whose blood flowed through my veins. There were no pictures of him lying around at home, his name never appeared on official documents, and Mother was vague about him. We were in dire straits, so she left for another country for work.

A few weeks had passed, and I found out that Ted Burlington, a business tycoon, needed a maid, so I jumped at the chance. Within days, I found myself sitting on an expensive leather couch. I listened attentively as the stern woman who greeted me, Mrs. Johnson, listed a mouthful of tasks that were expected to be completed while I was on the job. My eyes could not help but wander and take in the interior of the house. A lustrous chandelier hung from the gilded ceiling, its aureate borders gleaming. Then I felt something soft land on my covered lap – my uniform.

The next few days in the manor, I slogged and slaved without respite, overwrought. After a week, Mrs. Johnson strangely chose me to do the room- the master bedroom. The other maids looked at me green with envy as I fastidiously cleaned his room. However, it turned out to be a horrendous job, and she made it a living hell. She would reprimand me for even the smallest error and made me redo everything even when it took hours to complete. She drove me insane! She was nitpicking and relentless. She would also pass racist remarks, making me well up. Despite all that, I could not stop working as I needed the job so badly.

One fine day, just a few weeks after I had been working there, Mrs. Johnson warned me not to go in as the master was returning from his tedious business trip. We all lined up to greet him, and as soon as the lush limousine drove up over the gravel stones, he got down, and we greeted him briefly one by one. All of a sudden, as he was about to enter the door, he made a turn and stared at me but quickly dashed into the house after that. My cheeks heated up, and a bright shade of crimson red masked my face as accusatory eyes trained on me. After that, he whispered something to Mrs. Johnson, and she proceeded to make her way to me with a perplexed look. Then she beckoned for me to follow her. Bewildered, I followed her hesitantly to the doors of the master bedroom.

The man invited me to sit with him, but my mind was swirling. He took out a box to show me a picture of my Mother 20 years ago. He then asked if I knew this woman with a cautious tone. Nodding vigorously, I blurted that it was my Mother. His eyes softened, but mine widened as the realisation hit me that the man sitting before me was indeed my father.

We conversed for hours, piecing the pieces together and coming to the conclusion that Mrs. Johnson had sacked my Mother abruptly when she found out that she was pregnant. She was 'trying' to protect my father from the threat of a potential scandal. He was incensed because that was his decision, not hers. In fact, he was furious to discover what she had done. He embraced me as it finally dawned on him that I was his only daughter and heir. I looked forward to what the future was going to hold for me.

Then we heard some footsteps outside the oak door. It sounded like a lady, but then there were several sharp raps. I felt flustered and quickly stood up in fear of my superior. He calmed me down and opened the door. She gave me a disgusted look, and her eyes pierced my soul. I excused myself, leaving him to explain, but I heard him say, "You're fired!"

24. SIGATOKA

"Please work, please work!" I whispered frantically, raising my handheld device up to the sky. Internally, I was tormented and in turmoil at the notification 'No Signal' as it popped up, and that made me spiral into a frenzied state. It had only been a couple of hours, and my sanity was speedily making a break for it.

I had no food, a limited supply of water, no tent, and still no signal. I slumped back against the aged tree behind me with a defeated sigh. If only I had stood my ground and refused to join my younger brother and his group of friends on their impromptu trip to an unforsaken place. I doubted that they had even noticed my disappearance since that was what they had been doing thus far. They did not share the fact that they had brought me far away from home.

The scorching hot afternoon Sun shone mercilessly down upon my weakening state, making me regret my decision to follow them. Drenched in perspiration, my breaths started to become deeper, and I felt my chest constrict painfully. It did not help matters that the large expanse of leaves above me, along with the tall, thick bark of the matured trees that cornered me, made my claustrophobia go haywire.

My mouth felt drier than the Sahara Desert, and my surroundings started to spin. 'Was I dying?' I thought to myself. I sighed tiredly and flopped to the ground, propping myself up against the gargantuan tree, giving in to the darkness and wondering if the unfamiliar voices that I was hearing were going to be my rescuers.

When I began to come to my senses, I was pleasantly surprised yet perplexed to feel the softness of what seemed to be a soft cloth under my throbbing head. I squinted at the light source that came from the lamp that hung directly above me and shielded my eyes with my forearm. I began to sit up when I heard a woman's voice: "Don't even think about it, boy. Chief won't be very pleased with you if you do." I groaned, bringing my hand to my head when the dull throbbing in my head turned into a sharp pain. I turned my head slowly to look at the owner of the voice.

An array of vibrantly coloured feathers fanned out beautifully around the circumference of a carefully crafted wooden headdress that sat perfectly atop the head of a tall, stern-looking woman. She wore a gorgeous, burgundy, ankle-length dress that had a neckline adorned in small, black beads and an assortment of both chunky and dainty jewellery pieces on her wrists and fingers.

"Who are you, and where am I?" I asked. My voice was rough and croaky, making me frown and cough dryly. "A cup of water…here." The woman said, ignoring my question. I heard the hint of an accent, one I couldn't quite decipher. "Thanks," I muttered, grabbing the copper mug off the bedside table, and drinking from it greedily.

The woman began. "My husband and his men stumbled upon your dehydrated and delirious state. They've left me in charge of seeing to you. We are villagers of Sigatoka." I was baffled but in debilitating pain and could not fathom anything. Though, upon contemplation, that name sounded so familiar.

There was a square-shaped window beside the bed that I rested on that welcomed the dull, ochre glow of the evening Sun. I let my mind wander as I continued to gaze tiredly out the window. "I'll be back later tonight to clean up your wounds," Jonna said, advancing towards the doorway. She was extremely fixated on every blemish that I had, which made me wonder. My eyes glazed over as I hummed drowsily. With a sigh, I let my gaze focus on a dark spot in a far corner of the room.

As the Sun began to set, the direction of its rays slowly started to illuminate whatever that had been hiding. My breath hitched in my throat, and the all-too-familiar anxious feelings started spreading rapidly in my chest. Suddenly, I was wide awake. Slowly, the light from the window shone on a pile of what seemed like hard, shiny porcelain objects. I peered intently but was aghast to slowly realise that they were human bones that sat unsettlingly on a shelf, paraded like a trophy above a gory tiger skin rug! That's when it clicked: the last name- the bones- the village.

A few months ago, I watched a very intriguing documentary about this village. A cold chill ran down my spine, and I tried not to panic. Cannibals!

25. NO USE

Paralysed with trepidation, trauma, and turmoil, I could not command my legs to run. I stood rooted to the ground as the blood from my face rose to the surface. My lips split, and the metallic tang of blood lingered on my tongue. I stared into his charcoal eyes, and tears trickled down my face. Punches and kicks were thrown incessantly at me, and my body screamed in agony. Was I a punching bag? Unable to muster the strength to stand, my movements were jerky and autonomous. "Please stop, p..pl..please!" I pleaded, knowing fully well what was in store for me. My Mother-in-law spat and waved her finger at me while releasing a tirade of negative words in Hindi before making her way upstairs. At the corner of my eyes, I spotted my father-in-law, who was spectating powerlessly. His head was drooped so low that it looked as if he was lifeless. At that moment, I felt my whole world collapsing before me.

Growing up in a standard, strict Indian family, I had my life planned out by the age of 10. I would get married by the age of 16 and live with my husband's family. From that day onwards, my parents might as well be dead as I would never see them again. We lived in a small village. My father was a man in severe debt, and my Mother was a simple housewife. We didn't have money, just a roof over our heads and rice on the table. Aunty Mala, Rohan's Mother, was my father's boss. He was only their gardener but had promised her presents and jewellery if her son married me.

After months of applying for loans and working extra hours, the wedding was finally about to happen. I will forever remember the look on my parent's faces as I said my last goodbyes. "Pyaar karti hoon," I said as I lifted my draped saree off the ground and never looked back. "I love you."

"Ring Ring! Ring Ring!" The sound of my alarm at 4 am woke me from my slumber. I did my usual routine, which consisted of cooking breakfast, lunch and dinner, cleaning and ensuring that all menial tasks were completed. I then made sure I cleaned all the windows and folded the laundry. Staring at my reflection, I noticed the dark circles and bruises. This had been going on for four months now. So much so that I forgot who I really was behind the puffy eyes and pale skin. Rakesh made his way downstairs, reeking with alcohol, and I grimaced at the thought of him hurting me again. Avoiding a conversation, I quickly cleaned up and headed to prepare the ingredients for lunch. I felt embarrassed that my father couldn't pay my dowry. Shouldn't Rakesh have married me because he cared for me and not because he was doing a favour for my family by taking a female off their hands- a burden- from my father? He smirked and muttered incoherently, then pushed me aside. Yet again, he demanded the delayed payment of the dowry. I pleaded to him, but he guffawed and huffed, saying that I had reached the end of the rope.

That afternoon, I found my father-in-law in tears as he warned me that they would stoop low in order to accomplish what they had planned. My heart shattered. Both his son and wife had gone out to find some things to use against me. He confessed their evil plots and revealed that they were so despicable that they would consider terminating my existence. Devastated, I cried out to all the gods about my grievances. Calling my parents would be a futile solution.

Then they returned. Without flinching, he began a rampage against me; he dashed towards the altar and picked up a metal statue and grabbed a hold of my crowning glory. He told me that my parents had cheated them by not delivering what they had promised! He said that I was a despicable mistake. So, he had every right to 'terminate' this marriage.

I was speechless and dumbfounded. I wracked my brain, wondering how they could resort to such heinous actions. After all, I was going to be the Mother of his child. Instead, I was met with a massive blow on my head. Apprehensive as I was about my next move, I clambered up, using the coffee table to support me. But I fell back again.

My mind could not comprehend what was happening. The last thing I remember was a thin plastic covering my head. They were holding down my limbs and tied my hands with ropes they had just purchased. The blows numbed me, ensuring that all my breath would be snuffed out. Slowly drifting off into unconsciousness, I felt justified in putting rat poison in their *dhall sambar. That very morning.*

A smirk ran across my lips just before I heard my Mother-in-law regurgitating uncontrollably.

26. BROTHERS

Patrick and James were inseparable twin brothers, but not the kind you see in movies with identical looks and matching personalities. They were different and unique in their own right. Their bond was unbreakable, and they spent most of their days exploring the nooks and crannies of their house, a sprawling old mansion with creaky floors and hidden passages. Beyond the fence, however, was strictly off-limits, a rule imposed by their strict parents.

Patrick would always ask James, "What game shall we play together now, James?" They would then pretend to be bandits and run about gleefully. One day, while playing in their overgrown backyard, they noticed a young boy watching them from a distance. He was around their age, with jet-black hair that strangely shimmered in the sunlight and eyes as blue as the emerald sea, mirroring Patrick's own. His gaze was intense, yet there was a curious blankness in his expression that intrigued the twins. Despite his silent presence, he never ventured closer, content to remain an observer to their games.

As days turned into weeks, the boy's distant presence became more pronounced, his gaze a constant, unwavering look that seemed to follow the twins wherever they roamed. Intrigued by this enigmatic observer, Patrick and James found their curiosity piqued, until one day, they could resist it no longer. With a mixture of trepidation and excitement, they approached the boy, extending an invitation to join their games. The boy accepted, but on one condition: they must follow him into the dense, shadowed woods beyond the forbidden fence.

Ignoring the warnings echoing in their minds, Patrick and James followed the boy into the depths of the woods on a day when their parents were called away for an urgent meeting leaving them to their own devices. The trees towered overhead, their branches reaching out like gnarled fingers, casting eerie shadows on the forest floor. As they ventured deeper, the woods grew denser, the air thick with a sense of foreboding. After what felt like an eternity of walking, they emerged into a clearing where a dilapidated cottage stood, its once grand facade now weathered and worn. The windows were boarded up, and the walls were covered in ivy.

As the boy led them inside, a chill ran down Patrick's spine as they crossed the threshold.

The interior of the cottage was cloaked in darkness, the musty air thick with a sense of unease that made their skin crawl. Ignoring their apprehension, the boy began to taunt them with food, but what he presented to them was a revolting sight - a putrid, rotting mass that turned their stomachs and sent a wave of nausea washing over them.

Petrified with fear, Patrick and James tried to flee, but the boy's gaze seemed to pierce through them, freezing them in place. They were transfixed, unable to look away as the boy took a bite of the rotten flesh, his eyes flashing crimson in the dim light. The sight was horrifying, and a sense of dread washed over them as they realised the true nature of the boy they had followed into the woods.

Realising they were in grave danger, the twins made a desperate attempt to escape. Despite their panic state, they bolted out the door into the forest. As they sprinted, they turned to see him at their heels. In their haste, they failed to see roots jutting out from the ground, so they stumbled and fell into a ravine. Desperately clawing his way out, James yelled out to Patrick, beckoning him to follow suit. With a surge of adrenaline, James finally managed to climb out of the ravine and run towards home. He heard

Patrick's footsteps right behind him only a few metres away.

At last, the front door was right in front of them, and both dashed in, closing the door behind them. James bolted the door tightly, feeling relieved. While gasping for breath, he asked Patrick if he had hurt himself. Just then, as James turned towards his brother, he realised it wasn't his brother who had followed him home. It was the boy whose face twisted then into a sinister grin. "What game shall we play together now, James?" he mimicked Patrick hoarsely.

27. DELIGHTS CAN TURN SOUR

Two months ago, I bought a café with a picturesque view up in the mountains of Sichuan, southwestern Chinese province. A minuscule wooden café was built to serve customers. The Chinese café is swarmed with lively colossal trees coloured in dark chartreuse with a hunky healthy trunk and gargantuan mountains where birds are able to chirp and soar their wings around the vicinity. Clouds with enigmatic shapes filled the azure sky, depicting an elusive image of an idyllic atmosphere.

After hiring a professional chef, Meng Hua, our café business was thriving. Hikers and tourists would frequently visit the famous café, specifically for the food. My better half, Xin Yi and I were elated and confident about our investment. She was busy working as an accountant and hardly ever came by, but she was extremely supportive. I spent hours in the café, but she was extremely understanding and did my accounts perfectly.

The famous 'Mala noodles with *siew yoke*' was the best seller; it is a fresh hand-made light yellow noodles submerged in a numbing spicy broth that resplends a ruby colour. After a month of the café flourishing, a food inspector by the government was required as a routine. The day the food inspector came, it was a closed day in the café. A burly man with a shiny bald head entered the entrance of the café under a large board with the café's name written in a bold, exuberant font coloured golden. The husky man barged into the dining area, grasping onto a wooden cupboard with several printed slip papers. He then proceeded to examine the pulchritudinous interior design of the café and then advanced to the steely kitchen. The inscrutable inspector then went to place a mineral bine latex glove onto his stubby hands and began examining the inventory. He then opened the sturdy metal fridge to see covered pots that were abundant. He then stared into the pot after lifting the lid in an uncanny manner. He abruptly fished out his phone from his pocket and made a discreet phone call.

Ten minutes later, clamorous sirens with flashing red and bike lights appeared at the front of the café. My breathing started to intensify as my heart palpated against my ribs. Beads of perspiration formed at the top of my head. Two police officers gushed through the entrance of the door with metal handcuffs clinking as they walked. Little did I know those handcuffs were wrapped around my wrists. The officer forcefully pushed me out of the café and into the police car.

Thrown into jail, I had to spend the night in a cell that reeked of a malodorous stench of rat urine that permeated through the air. Sleeping on the prison bed that had pillow covers that were as hard as sandpaper made it difficult to sleep. Suddenly, without anticipation, the cell guard hollered at me to get up - I had a visitor. Being let through the perpetual corridors came a room with tables and chairs, and Meng was sitting on one of those tables, so I bellowed his name in ecstasy.

I started to yammer about how ridiculous this predicament was. Meng then blatantly confessed that what the inspector saw inside was an unidentified questionable meat bought off the black market using my credit card. This was so that I could lose my café. Out of perplexity, I gave him a forlorn look in agony. He then admitted that his first true love had left him abruptly for another man. Her name was Xin Yi.

28. THE UNKNOWN SHOULD NEVER BE VENTURED

A hug of browns, a shelter of extended limbs, seven resting beneath foliage hues, the forest is a protective Mother, the promise of the holy sanctuary. The forest silenced the clocks, for this place of root and branch is the dominion of the eternal soul. Suzanna toddled with a full basket of fresh glistening red apples on the fallen dried leaves along the harmony that the lovely birds chirped. The Sun began to fall into a deep slumber while the gloomy moon appeared lazily to interchange their shifts. Her five senses were desperately telling her that she was not heading in the right direction. Nonetheless, it was beyond tardy the moment she acknowledged it.

Suzanna panicked with terror, apprehensively searching around for any familiar sight, but the irksome darkness averted her mercilessly. "Mother must be worried," she thought guiltily to herself as she anxiously bit her muddy nails in an attempt to simmer down. A small wound materialised under her relentless biting and soon released the alluring scent of fresh, sweet, youthful, scarlet fluid. "Ow!" She groaned at the stingy pain coming from her ring finger nail and immediately wiped it on her pearl white dress. Hours of creepy, chilling, and freaking tree trunks and the fluttering of wings unseen while the grass slid against her pant legs with reverberating breathing sounds simply left her with scarcely any energy left to run. Regardless of the fear of uncertainty, Susan still insisted to continue heading the front as she remembered the consequences of staying out in the woods late at night.

Out of the blue, Suzanna caught sight of a familiar crowd of pine trees that she planted with the villagers decades ago as a barrier to their existence from the outside world. "The real world is where the real monsters are," Suzanna's Mother, the head chief, always told her that. She darted into the antique wooden hut that grew from the ground as an ancient seed of the primordial search. She searched around but could not find any signs of her Mother and thought that she went out to find her. Mass hysteria erupted in her as it was the dead of the night, where nocturnal creatures are awakened by the calls of spirit, and no one in the village was allowed to go out at such a time. The villagers warned, at the end of the forest, concealed the cataclysmic side of black magic where the witches lived in seclusion, hidden inside ghastly caves, ready to hunt down the disobedient villagers for their blood that can once revitalise youth. Nevertheless, the effect does not last long. Consequently, the prey for humans does not end.

Subsequently, she plodded back into the caliginous woods to trace for her Mother's footsteps. She dug in deeper and deeper, slowly reaching the atrocious side of the village without noticing the danger that she had gotten herself in. She noticed many endless caves, lit indistinctly. The cacophony sounds of toads made her more vigilant about her surroundings. A swift movement behind promptly caught her attention. She hastily turned around and saw a woman, aged like her Mother, standing not far away from her. She froze with terror, unable to move, while shivers ran down her spine. "Mother?" she piled her remaining courage and questioned carefully. The woman did not speak but hobbled towards her soundlessly. She trembled and took a step back. "Mother, is that you?" she bellowed with all her might, with the last hope. With no responses received, Suzanna spurted instantaneously into a cold sweat. The woman chased after her unceasingly. Suzanna looked behind and quivered as the scrawny woman got closer and closer behind her and ran with all her hands and legs like a giant spider. It was visible that she yearned for fresh human blood for her sunken eyes and wrinkled face.

"Thud!" a big leap from the woman landed on her. She tried to avoid the woman's attack but was held captivated by her sturdy limbs. "I told you not to leave the village at midnight," a benevolent and familiar tone coaxed. Suzanna craned her neck for a closer look. The same scar on her Mother's hand appeared on the woman. BUT IT WAS ON THE WRONG HAND!

Suddenly, she turned her benign face into pure turpitude and snarled like a wicked snake, showing its fierce, ferocious, and feral fangs, ready to pounce! An ear-busting scream reverberated through the air, but the forest soon regained its odd serenity a few moments later. This old-growth forest was a tunnel into another time, a place where it could be any century, and no one would ever know you left, nor anyone you left there.

29. THE MISSION-POSSIBLE

A mission was passed to us from Mr. Robinson, the well-known scientist whose father once discovered a medicine to cure degenerative cells but passed away because he could not defy old age. So, a group of three researchers were summoned to find one of the rarest species known to mankind and bring it back to thc laboratory. This was only discovered in the deadliest old-growth forest located in southeast Asia. The risks were even higher when both of my teammates did not like each other. Nonetheless, the boss could not resist the alluring return of a great deal of cash. Apart from that, the university would benefit from a handsome reward, too.

Soon, a small helicopter left us inside the forest and told us to meet there again after it was time for the pick-up. I took a wooden stick and carved a cross on the pine tree as a remark. Immediately afterwards, we promptly started our journey with only limited time left in our hands.

The trees in the old forest were nicotine-brown. Orcs were gobbling meat and grinding on bones.

Gloomy scrubs hid dangerous creatures. The musty air was difficult to breathe. The forest was old and antiquated. Oxblood-red toadstools littered the ground where poisonous cowbane grew next to them. An acrid odour hung off everything. I anxiously bit my tongue as a release of nervousness and the fishy, metallic taste of scarlet fluid filled my mouth. We desperately followed the map in our hands while detailedly scanning around us for any possible danger, and soon tried to control the thrill of reaching our destination: the most hidden spot in the forest, the only place to spot the unrivalled, unequalled and unsurpassed plant that can potentially replenish anyone's youth.

With some pictures and detailed research given to us as a reference, we began our miserable search for the plant, which seemed to be playing hide-and-seek with us. This part of the forest was nut-brown and much more primitive. The trees were towers of the forest. In front of us sat the magnificent aquarium-blue waterfall that was drizzling onto the rocks. It looked like a wall of blue satin threaded with silver. At its widest point, it was surging and plunging down the mountain. "This is the perfect spot." I thought soundlessly to myself. The flowers next to it were nodding gently. A loud "thud" soon interrupted my fascination, along with splashes of water. "Ow!" Tabitha groaned in pain while Stan jeered mercilessly. The two girls started relentless bickering while I sighed weakly, still looking for the 'treasure.'

"It's here!" Tabitha bellowed all of a sudden breathlessly. I turned around with exhilaration and saw both Tabitha and Stan trying to balance themselves at the waterfall's widest point with their hands holding the invaluable miracle. They handed over the plant to me to examine. With a positive result of the test, they cheered merrily. Once I had it in my possession, I blurted out, "Look there, there's more in front!" They greedily turned around, oblivious to what was going to happen next. Without a second thought, I forcefully pushed them down the waterfall. Screeching screams rang resoundingly and intruded the tranquillity of the forest, but its serenity soon returned to its impenetrable state. "It's all mine now," I smirked jubilantly with a plan to explain their demise, claiming that a beast had arisen from the forest and devoured them!

After a few hours, the helicopter came to the pick-up spot. It threw out a long rope for me to climb onto. I strenuously gripped onto it and ascended with struggle. "Hand me the bag!" Mr Robinson hollered, grinning from ear to ear before I could give a feeble excuse for my missing teammates. He had an avaricious look that made me feel perplexed.

Nevertheless, I enthusiastically passed over my bag and was ready for him to pull me up by my arm. Out of the blue, I felt the rope becoming loosened. I looked to my right, and my heart dropped. A man was about to let go of the rope, intending to drop me down. "Mr. Robinson, help!" I blustered out. A wicked grin split across his wrinkled face. "You fool! It's worth much more than you think, and I'm not about to begin to share it with you," he expressed while egocentrically touching his crested, crinkled and crumbly skin.

With the lacking grip of the loosened rope, I screamed. I had my eyes opened for a while but closed them, feeling no use in having them open since I could not see anything. I felt the strong wind compressing me and pushing me down. My whole body was falling in darkness towards large looming trees. Mr. Robinson never planned to share his reward with anyone. I finally understood what tasting my own medicine meant.

30. WHY

In the quiet dawn, a girl named Emma stirred from her slumber, the remnants of a forgotten dream lingering in her mind. She slowly got ready for school and descended the stairs of her old house in unison, with the familiar creaks and groans echoing through the empty rooms. Her Mother sat at the kitchen table, lost in a world of her own making, a faint scent of something bitter in the air. Emma felt exasperated because, over the past few weeks, she had been negligent. She stopped caring. Emma was distraught at the thought of a Mother who cared more about wallowing in self-pity than caring about her only child! Alcohol engulfed her now, and Emma's gentle pleas and calls to her were met with only inconsolable tears from her and more gulps of the alcohol. So much so that she stopped trying. Her father had long since vanished, leaving behind a void that seemed to grow with each passing day.

Emma, an only child, wandered through the shadows of her solitude, the weight of her loneliness pressing down on her shoulders like a heavy shroud. Outside, the tantalising aroma of waffles wafted from the neighbour's house, a stark contrast to the desolation within her own home. Hurrying down the street, the late hour threatened her punctuality for school. In the distance, she spotted her friend, Danielle, who seemed lost lately in her own melancholic world, dressed in a gothic dark ensemble that spoke volumes of her inner turmoil. Emma quickened her pace, hoping to catch up and offer some semblance of comfort in the midst of Danielle's storm.

Desperate to lift Danielle's spirits, Emma engaged her in chatter about their favourite music artists, hoping to draw a smile from her friend's sombre face. Slowly, a glimmer of joy flickered in Danielle's eyes, a fleeting moment of respite from the darkness that surrounded her. As they walked, Emma felt a sense of warmth and connection, a reminder that even in the darkest of times, friendship could be a beacon of light.

As they reached the school grounds, the whispers of judgement and ridicule followed them, labelling Danielle as 'mental.' Unable to bear the cruelty, Emma broke away and sought solace in the school restroom, where her tears flowed freely. The weight of the world seemed to crush her, the harsh words of her peers echoing in her mind like a relentless drumbeat.

Emma followed right behind her with her head down, in case they made fun of her too, as her attire was not exactly 'peer friendly.' Danielle bawled like she had never before, and Emma tried to pry carefully about why she had become so disconsolate and disconnected recently. She raised her head up from her palms and stared at her incredulously. "Do you still not know why I am acting this way?" Emma shook her head from left to right slowly yet panicking because of her volatile and erratic behaviour.

Then she got up and told me to meet her at our favourite spot after school, where she would reveal the truth about everything that had happened to her. Emma gladly submitted, wanting to find out the root of the problem. It wasn't long before the bell rang, and they made their way to the old oak tree in the dark spruce woods. That was their place to exchange stories and tell each other their hopes and dreams. The area was secluded, and no one knew about it. Layers of fallen pine needles and sentinels were strewn on the bronze-coloured earth. Emma became perplexed when she didn't stop walking after seeing the oak tree.

Danielle's mannerisms and demeanour restricted Emma from prying, so she just ambled on, though Emma must admit, feeling a little exhilarated at the thought of perhaps a new place for them to gossip. As she marched deeper and deeper down the winding path, Emma began to feel exhausted and started to notice the rustle of some animals scurrying and scuttling amidst the swaying of the trees with the wind. The emerald-coloured leaves and yellowish branches lashed and interweaved against each other as if they were prompting the forest about our intrusion. They leaned toward each other, black and ominous, in the fading light. A vast silence reigned as Emma began to shiver and tremble; cold crept up. She wanted to stop Danielle, but she looked like she was adamant about what she wanted to do.

Soon, they arrived at an open spot. Lo and behold. There were large stones, and she traced her pointed finger to one large newly dug-up spot. The stone had a name. It read 'Emma Palmer.' "That's my name!" she blurted out.

"Yes, Emma. You died in a car accident a few weeks ago. You were on the way home on the only day that I was absent. I wasn't there for you." she sobbed. "But… but… I think it's time for you to go." Finally, Emma realised why her Mother had been ignoring her. She was sad but understood. Danielle held their picture tightly, taking one last look at their beautiful friendship and waved, indicating that it was her way of bidding farewell. The cold was wearing off, and slowly, Emma waved back to say goodbye and began to disappear as she drifted off with the wind.

www.ingramcontent.com/pod-product-compliance
Lightning Source LLC
LaVergne TN
LVHW091101150826
845673LV00002B/679

* 9 7 9 8 8 9 3 2 2 8 7 3 1 *